NO
TOMORROW

NO TOMORROW

Jake Hinkson

NEW PULP PRESS

Published by New Pulp Press, LLC, 926 Truman Avenue,
Key West, Florida 33040, USA.

For information contact:
Publisher@NewPulpPress.com

ISBN-13:978-0692524275 (New Pulp Press)
ISBN-10: 0692524274

For
Gin Armstrong

"Meaningless! Meaningless!" saith the Preacher. "Everything is meaningless!"

- Ecclesiastes 1:2

"There's no road back. There're no yesterdays.There's no tomorrow. There's only today.Everyday you live is a day before you die."

- Crashout (1952)

NO
TOMORROW

Part One: The Woman From Hollywood

Summer, 1947

Chapter One

"Don't go to Arkansas," the theater owner in Kansas City told me.

I was unloading canisters of a picture called *Secrets of a Sorority Girl* from the back of my car. I stood up straight and said, "What?"

The old man leaned through the backdoor of his theater and spit some tobacco in the general direction of a trash bin. "Didn't you say you was headed down to the Ozarks?"

"Yeah, that's my next stop."

The old timer scratched his chin. "Well, you should steer clear of Arkansas. A girl all alone down there could get herself in trouble."

I just smiled at that as he passed me the canisters of a Lash Lu Rue western called *Ghost Town Renegades*.

As I wedged them into the crowded back of the car, he asked, "You ever been down there?"

"No, this is my first trip."

He shook his head. "Well, let me tell you, it's a whole different world, Billie. It's where the Midwest ends and the South begins, and that transition ain't pretty."

"I heard it was lovely country."

"Ain't the country I'm talking about. The further down into the Ozarks you go, the more peculiar the people get. You'll be okay as long as you're in Missouri, but you watch yourself once you get to Arkansas. They ain't got proper dispositions down there."

"Aw, c'mon. The Ozarks are the Ozarks, right?"

He looked at me like I'd spit on the Missouri state

flag. "Them hillbillies in Arkansas are meaner than a mess of snakes. Had a uncle went down there in 1913. Ain't heard from him since."

I laughed at that, and he allowed himself a little smile.

I said, "Dick Powell is from Arkansas."

"Is that a fact?"

"I think so. Seems like I read it in a movie magazine, anyway. He and Alan Ladd both are from there, I think."

"Well, the Ozarks ain't populated by a bunch of movie stars. You just remember that."

"All right," I assured him. "I'll be careful."

We shook hands, and I climbed into the company car. It was a '41 Mercury station wagon, with scratched wooden doors and my suitcase crammed into the back between heaps of film canisters. As I pulled out of the alley, I gave him a wave.

Heading south, I didn't worry about the old timer's warning. Although I had been PRC's mid-South distribution agent for only a few weeks, I'd already figured out that one hick town was about as bad as all the others. As I slipped out of the city and back into the open country, I cursed myself again for taking the job in the first place.

All things considered, I thought, *maybe I should have stuck with the writing.*

~ ~ ~

"The problem isn't that you're a woman," the man at PRC had told me. "The problem is we don't need another writer. Writers grow on palm trees out here. And, hell, most of our pictures write themselves, anyway."

"That's bad news for me," I said.

His office was a cramped hole at the back of PRC Studios, just one door down from the men's room, and his only window looked out on the side of another building five feet away. He leaned across his little desk and pushed back the writing samples I'd brought in.

I didn't reach for them. I just waited.

He had a tanned face and crooked teeth. He was lucky to have the bad teeth because otherwise he was as plain as a paper sack. An all points bulletin on him would just say: be on the lookout for a tanned studio flunky with crisscrossed incisors.

He asked, "Where're you from, Miss Dixon?"

"Call me Billie," I said.

"Where're you from originally, Billie?"

"Texas."

"Thought I heard a little cactus in that accent. How long you been in LA?"

"A few years."

"Move out here to break into the movies?"

I smiled. "No. Nothing fancy like that. I just wanted to get away from my grandmother's general store. Been refilling coffee cups over on Sunset for the last five years. Then last week my boss's niece got canned from Lockheed, so he fired me and gave her my job."

"That's tough."

"I decided to come down to the studios and look for work."

"You thought you could go from wiping counters to writing pictures just like that, huh?"

"Why not? Based on what I've seen, I can write one as well as the next gal. Besides, I'm a natural born liar, and as near as I can tell writing for the pictures is all about giving pretty people interesting things to say. What God shorted me in looks, he compensated me for in gab."

He smiled slightly at that, but I could tell he was thinking.

"You went to other studios before you came here?" he asked.

"Hey, I'm not going to lie to you," I said. "Sure I went to the big boys first. Who wouldn't?"

He nodded sadly. "Indeed. You talk your way into any meetings over at the big boys?"

"I got a couple of meetings. Warner Brothers. Fox."

"But ..."

"Nothing panned out."

"Mm. I bet. So you came over to Poverty Row."

"Girl needs to eat."

He nodded and lit a cigarette. "Know anything about this part of town?"

"What do you mean?"

"Poverty Row is Hollywood's toilet," he said. "We make six-reel pictures that have all the staying power of a roll of Scott Tissue. Every nickel and dime outfit up and down Gower Street follows pretty much the same business strategy. We shoot a picture for about twelve or fifteen grand, at the rate of about one a week, mostly as filler for double bills. This helps the theater owners convince their customers that they're getting two pictures for the price of one, when what they're really getting is a classy A-picture from the big studios followed by one of our B-grade pieces of shit." He regarded his cigarette and said, "Here's the thing, Billie. Like I said before, we don't really need another Goddamn writer. What we need is a field man."

"What's a field man do?" I asked.

"Well, some of these little theaters out there in the ass end of nowhere can't afford the big A-pictures. They only run the cheapest of the cheap stuff, sometimes years after it's come out. We get our movies out to most of them through states rights distributors and exchanges, but some of these theaters are so small or so out of the way we have to dispatch someone out there to peddle the stuff by hand. That's where the field man comes in. His job is to shovel the studio shit as far into the heartland as he can get it."

"You're hiring for this job?"

"Got an opening for the mid-South distribution agent. That would mean schlepping our wares out to hick towns in Missouri, Arkansas, and Tennessee, and trying to convince the local theater owner down there that he's getting a deal on some fifty-minute masterpiece like *Thundering Gunslingers*. These hick exhibitors usually take what they can get. The hours are brutal, and the pay is insulting. I never had a dame do it before, but you got spunk and personality." He looked at his watch. "And, hell, if I fill this position before noon I can go ahead and start drinking."

"Not exactly the job I had in mind when I walked in here."

He flashed me some bad teeth and laughed. "Hey, join the club. But if you want a job in the movie business, this is the one I can offer you."

~ ~ ~

My fancy Hollywood career.

At least it used to be.

That was before I got mixed up in this bad business in Arkansas. I can remember thinking that morning as I left Kansas City that my job – that my life, really – couldn't get much worse. Looking back now, that makes me laugh. It really makes me laugh.

Chapter Two

The Midwest unravels into the Ozarks. Fields, which begin as green and as flat as pool tables, gradually rise on either side of the road before they give way to thickly wooded hills punctured by rocky outcroppings. The further I descended into the Ozarks, the more impulsively the roads wound through the trees, as if they were following the weavings of a drunk man. Twisted, half-assed paths clung to the side of piney highlands, and although I had a map on the seat next to me, I couldn't look at it and drive at the same time for fear of hurtling over the edge of a fifty-foot ravine. By the time I hit Arkansas I was white-knuckling the steering wheel and cursing the whole damn business.

I actually sighed with relief when I made one last turn around a bend and found myself unexpectedly in Stock's Settlement. Spread across a green valley between two stubby mountains, the dirt road town hugged the Clear Water River on the west and climbed up a little hill to the east. In the center of the town square, a three story courthouse towered over the cluster of little shops and diners that surrounded it.

I found the Eureka Theater at the end of Main Street. It was hard to miss. Though it had probably been built before the talkies took off, besides the courthouse it was still the nicest building I'd seen in town. It had a brown Beaux-Arts façade and a sign out front advertising air conditioning. Still, it was clearly in disrepair. The marquee looked as if it had been raided for aluminum at some point during the war and never quite replaced.

I checked my hair and makeup, smoothed down

my skirt, and got out of the car. As I walked up to the box office I saw a small handwritten sign that read:

Our Air Conditioning Is Still Broke

I walked past the box office and tried to peer through the glass portholes in the front doors. No lights appeared to be on in the place, although enough sunlight slipped through that I could tell it wasn't abandoned or covered in dust. I knocked on the front door, but no one answered. I went back to the box office and saw that the theater had no show times listed.

I walked around the side of the building and found a door propped open with a wedge of wood. Before I could step inside, a chicken walked out.

"Jesus Christ," I muttered.

I leaned in the darkened door and called "Hello! Anybody here besides this chicken?"

The sweltering theater could probably seat a hundred people on the floor and fifty in the balcony, but it lay fallow and smelled of live poultry and old cigars.

Presently, the lobby door opened and a man walked out.

He was a little fellow, hunchbacked and cockeyed, with a cigar protruding from a thicket of red whiskers.

"Howdy," he said in a rough squeak of a voice as he hobbled down the aisle.

"Howdy. You the proprietor of this establishment?"

"I reckon."

"I'm Billie Dixon."

"Billie?"

"Yes sir."

He held out a knotty hand. "Claude Jeter."

We shook, and I said, "Nice to meet you, Mr.

Jeter. I'm from the Producer's Releasing Corporation, and I'm here to make you a deal on some fine motion pictures. I have a selection of films with me, and I have complete listings on our new and upcoming releases."

Jeter squinted at me behind his cigar and said, "Fine motion pictures? You new at this, ma'am?"

I lied to him with a smile. "No sir. I've been at it for a few years now."

"Well, unless PRC changed hands, I can't figure that their pictures got no better."

The darkened theater was hot as all hell, but Jeter stood there sucking on his cigar and squinting at me like he didn't notice.

"Well, at any rate," I said, "we got some new ones."

The old man lowered himself gradually into a theater seat and said, "Well, I'll tell you, I don't know as I need any more pictures no how."

Staying by the open door in the hope that a breeze would come along and cool me, I asked, "Why is that, Mr. Jeter?"

"You'n call me Claude," he said. For the first time he pulled the cigar out of his mouth. He blew off a half inch of ash, then stuck the cigar back into the center of his whiskers. "I'm thinking of shutting her on down."

"Folks around here don't like going to the pictures anymore?"

Claude said, "Well, no, it ain't that. I got a whole mess of problems. With the war over, a lot folks around here is out of work and ain't got the dime to spare on a movie ticket. Them that got the dime and a car drive on down to the Star Light Theater in Black Bear where they can see Gary Cooper and Ingrid Bergman movies. Of course, now that the Goddamn air conditioner is broke and I ain't got the money to get it fixed, I don't even got no cold air to offer. And truth be told, the customers like the air more than most of the pictures."

"I'm sorry to hear that. Maybe if I gave you one of our newest pic – "

"None of that matters, though. Because none of that is my number one problem."

"What's your number one problem?"

"My number one problem is the man of God who lives across the river there and runs the biggest church around has decided that motion pictures is the spawn of the devil."

"He's come out against you?"

"Well, sure, me and my portal to perdition." Claude laced his fingers together on his belly and pushed his legs into the aisle. "He means to put me out of bidness, and I reckon he's gonna do it, too. People around here think he's a regular Ozark Moses. A portion of them, anyways. A portion of them will do any damn thing he tells them. And if'n he tells not to go to the pictures, they stay away."

"Have you tried talking to him?"

Without moving his head, Claude puffed on his cigar. "I ain't about to go over there and talk at him and have him tell me I'm going to hell. I'd just as soon close down as do that."

The chicken walked up to the door and regarded me suspiciously.

"Hey," Claude said to me, "make way there for Franklin Roostervelt. He likes to come in and hunt for bugs."

I let the chicken, rooster, or whatever the hell it was come inside. I said, "Have you tried paying this preacher?"

"Pay him for what?"

I shrugged. "It wouldn't be the first time in the history of the motion picture industry that some moral crusader got paid to go away. Maybe he's waiting for you to make him an offer."

Claude watched Franklin Roostervelt peck at the floor.

"Never thought to offer him a deal," he said.

"Wouldn't be a bad idea."

"Might not. I ain't got a lot to offer. Maybe I could cut him in on a share under the table."

"He might like the extra income."

"He might at that."

I had a thought. "Say," I said moving into the theater, "how about I go over and talk to him?"

He perked up at that suggestion. "That'd be awful white of you, Billie."

"And in return, how about we make a deal on some movies?"

He settled back in his seat. "Oh."

"What? You need new pictures. I got new pictures. You take a couple off my hands, sign a deal for a couple more, and I'll go over there and talk to this preacher. You're back in business by tonight. Save up, get that air conditioning fixed. This place will be hopping like Grauman's Chinese Theater in no time."

Claude pulled out his cigar and blew off some ash. "Just not another Buster Crabbe western, for God's sake. I can't sit through another one of those. How about Bob Steele? You got any Bob Steele? I like him. He's got mean eyes."

"Yeah, I think I got some Bob Steele pictures. It's a deal then?"

"First you go talk to the preacher."

"Where do I find him?"

"The church, of course. Go across the river and up the hill."

I leaned over and we shook, and I was about to leave, but Claude said, "Just you watch how you talk to him, though."

I turned around at the door. "*How* I talk to him?"

"Yeah. He's meaner'n Bob Steele. And remember, to him, you been sent by the devil."

Chapter Three

A little past the river, just as the main road headed out of town, I turned up a stringy side path marked Church Hill Road. Snaking through the hills, I followed the road to a little bridge straddling a sparkling rivulet. On the other side, atop a green hillock sat a large wooden building with a flight of stone steps and a large sign out front that read: The Blood-Bought Baptist Tabernacle. I parked next to the sign and pulled a little round pocket mirror from my glove compartment. I was checking my hair when the front door of the church opened.

A man in a black suit with no tie or hat walked out. His eyes were closed. Even as I got out of the car, he didn't open his eyes or change his expression.

"Howdy, " I said.

"Howdy," he said in a pleasant rasp.

"Are you the preacher here?"

He walked down the steps, hands at his sides, but he still didn't open his eyes. "I'm Brother Obadiah Henshaw," he said. "Glad to know you, Miss ..."

"Billie Dixon," I said walking toward him and extending a hand.

Brother Obadiah Henshaw had cropped black hair on top of a high, wide forehead. He kept his eyes squeezed shut, and it took me a moment to realize the son of a bitch was blind.

"I suspect you just noticed something about me," he said.

"Yes sir."

"Lost my sight in the war. Lost my sight and saw the light. Never read scripture before the war, but the Lord sent a feller to read me the word while I was laid up in the ward. I memorized it all – the entire Bible – laying there on my back and listening to that feller read. One of these days, when I'm called to the final judgment, the Lord will restore my sight. The first thing I want to see is the face of my Lord Jesus. The second thing I want to see is them words. I just want to see them wonderful words."

I had a feeling that Brother Obadiah Henshaw had repeated that story many times.

He extended his hand in my general direction. When I met his hand, he gave me a shake that felt like he meant it. Holding on, he smiled and said, "What was your name again?"

"Billie Dixon."

"What's the Billie short for?"

"William, actually."

"You're a woman with a man's name?"

"Yes sir, that's my lot in life."

"Now, how'd that come to be?"

"I was named after my father. He ran out on my mother before I was born, and to get back at him, she gave me his name and then dumped me on his mama's doorstep."

Still holding onto my hand, Brother Henshaw said, "That's a peculiar thing for a woman to do."

"She was a peculiar woman. That's the story grandma told me, anyway."

The preacher finally let go of my hand.

"Where you from, Miss Dixon?" he asked, not unpleasantly.

"Well, sir, that's why I came up here to see you today. I'm from Hollywood, California, and I've been led to believe that you don't care much for the motion picture business. Is that fair to say?"

Now the preacher seemed to pull back. His heavy brow tightened as he turned his attention toward the sound of the water down the hill. "The Lord doesn't care much for the motion picture business, Miss Dixon. I just take my lead from him."

"Yes, sir. I respect that you feel that way. But I work for a fine company called Producer's Releasing Corporation. It specializes in wholesome family fare such as westerns. Now, I know we all love the stories of the American frontier, stories of the brave pioneer men who founded this country. I'm sure you can see how pictures like that can be a culturally edifying experience for the whole community."

"Culturally edifying?"

"Yes sir."

"Is that the end of what you got to say?"

"Well ..."

"Because I don't happen to agree with you, Miss Dixon. Seems to me that the California moving picture business is just a tool of Satan, a smoke-and-mirror show that he puts on to lure unsuspecting folks into all kinds of indecency. In this town, the movie theater is little more than a make-out place for wayward teenagers and local ne'er-do-wells. Those people on screen? Women paid to walk around in nightgowns and drink liquor and kiss men for money. Harlots, that's what the Bible calls those kinds of women."

While I was trying to think of what to say to that, he turned his shut eyes to me and said, "So I reckon you can go on back to Claude Jeter and tell him that he's gonna have to do more than send some Hollywood floozy out here to sweet talk me."

I dabbed my brow with a handkerchief. While I did, a side door to the church opened, and a woman stepped outside.

She was a looker. She wore a simple white blouse and a long brown skirt, but her unpinned hair hung about her shoulders in strawberry-blond curls and her thin eyebrows arched high over sleepy blue eyes. As she moved though the grass in her bare feet, she smiled politely and said, "I didn't realize we had a visitor."

"This is Miss Dixon from Hollywood," the preacher said. "Claude Jeter brought her all the way down here to set me straight on my theology."

I smiled. "I don't know if I'd put it exactly that way myself," I said. "But I am pleased to meet you ..."

She put out her hand, and as we shook I noticed a plain gold wedding band. "Amberly Henshaw," she said. There was something different in her bearing and voice – different from her husband, different from all I'd seen of the town of Stock's Settlement so far. She moved as gracefully as if she'd been to finishing school, and she pronounced her name with the crispness of someone who'd had elocution lessons.

"Mrs. Henshaw, it's so nice to meet you. I was just talking to your husband here about your conflict with nice old Mr. Jeter."

Mrs. Henshaw smiled at that. "Now, I'm afraid you'll have to do better than that, Miss Dixon. Claude Jeter is certainly old but he's not exactly nice. He doesn't have much use for people. Mostly he just sits around that theater of his smoking his cigars and playing with his rooster."

Brother Henshaw made a face like he tasted sour milk. "I can't abide that dirty old man."

His wife nodded. "I do miss going to the pictures, though. I haven't been in years. I used to go quite often, before the war."

Brother Henshaw murmured, "Mm. I'm sure that drunkards who give their lives to Christ sometimes miss the taste of whiskey."

She answered him. "Yes. I suppose they do."

Her husband nodded.

"Well," she said, "if you'll excuse me, I'm going down the hill to dip my feet in the water." A soft breeze lifted her hair and I caught the scent of her perfume. It was nice, and surprisingly strong. I wondered if the preacher – who seemed like the kind of man to impose austerity on his wife – allowed her to wear it because he liked the smell as a compensation for what he couldn't see.

Mrs. Henshaw smiled at me and shook my hand again. "Goodbye, Miss Dixon."

As I watched her walk down the hill, the preacher asked, "Are we done?"

"Sir?"

"Unless you want to ask Jesus Christ to become your personal Lord and savior, then I don't know what else we have to discuss."

I turned to him. "Well, there is one possibility we have not discussed."

"And what's that?"

"Mr. Jeter might be willing to make a faith offering to the church."

The preacher's lips curled up in something between contempt and amusement. "You trying to bribe me, girl?"

"Not at all. I'm merely pointing out that Claude – that Mr. Jeter would like to tithe a portion of his earnings to the church every week. He can't do that, however, if he's not permitted to earn a living."

The preacher laced his thick fingers together and bent them back and forth to crack his knuckles. "Funny thing ... I've railed agin drink as much as I ever railed agin pictures, but I never once had a shiner offer to cut me in on the proceeds."

"I – "

The preacher stepped toward me, his head lowered like a bull's. "I think you better scoot on down

17

the road, missy, before me and the Lord learn you about the wages of sin."

I held up my hands. "No need to get pugilistic, Brother Henshaw. I can take no for an answer. Thank you for your time."

I went back to my car, fired it up and backed out of there.

I headed down the hill, cursing the job as never before. Arkansas preachers and movie theater roosters. I dreaded to see what Tennessee had in store for me. As I neared the bottom of the hill, I saw Amberly Henshaw with her feet in the water, her face lifted to the sun. As I approached the bridge, she opened her eyes and looked back up the hill. Her husband had gone back inside.

She stepped out of the water and waved me down.

I slammed on the brakes and the car slid ten feet down the gravel road as a curtain of dust swept over us.

She ran up to the car, her faced flushed with sun and dotted with sweat. "Tomorrow," she said. "He's going visiting after lunch."

"What? I don't ... I hadn't planned to stay the night in town."

She shrugged as if it didn't make the least difference one way or another. "Then don't," she said. "But he's going visiting tomorrow after lunch, and I'm staying here."

Without saying anything else, she turned and walked back down to the water. I looked up the hill at the church. Then I put the car in drive and headed for the movie theater.

As I drove, I kept hearing Amberly Henshaw's crisp voice saying, "Tomorrow."

What did she want from me? Why did she want me to come see her? Could she take one look at me and tell?

No one in Texas ever spoke out loud about such things, of course, but I noticed that once I hit puberty and prettied up a bit, along with the inevitable male attention came one miserable-looking housewife who lingered too long at my grandmother's store to talk to me. One night, she stopped me after work, calling to me from the driver's seat of her husband's car. She stepped out, her mouth trembling as she tried to say my name. Then she started to cry and ran back to the car. She drove away, and I never saw her again.

My first week in Los Angeles I met a shorthaired factory girl who took me to the Well Well Club on La Brea. It was a world I hadn't even dreamed of. Girls in jeans and work shirts dancing with dames in heels and skirts. It was a hell of a time for me. I dressed like Marlene Dietrich and bedded secretaries and servicemen's wives. It was fun, but nothing ever stuck. Dodging police raids was bad enough – I still have the scar where I sliced open my hand crawling out the bathroom window one Friday night – but dealing with dames was even worse. People just had too much to lose. Families. Careers. They all went back to their boyfriends or their husbands. They settled, and then they settled down. I'd seen more than one old flame pushing a stroller down the street.

But this redneck preacher's well-spoken wife was a whole other prospect completely. I wasn't a damn fool. I knew where I was. I knew I had no business going to see her.

"Tomorrow," she'd said and looked me in the eye.

Tomorrow. I couldn't remember the last time that word had held much promise, but now I couldn't get it out of my mind.

Tomorrow.

I didn't go back to the movie theater right away. I stopped down the street and checked into Stock's Settlement's only motor lodge.

19

Chapter Four

That night, the Eureka Theater opened for business. I gave Claude a mystery picture called *Strange Illusion* to run. The thing was a couple years old, and it didn't make a damn bit of sense, but it was spooky and queer enough to keep you interested. I thought it was one of our better pictures, actually.

An hour before show time I went up in the booth with him to load it.

"Say," I said, "what's the deal with the preacher's wife?"

Claude unspooled one of the reels onto a big platter behind the projector. He grinned at me behind his smoke and whiskers. "You met Sister Amberly, huh?"

I smiled back at him. "I sure did. She's a treat."

"Awful pretty girl, that's for sure. Beauty queen from Missouri."

"Beauty queen?"

"Yeah Miss Something-or-Other. I don't guess anyone around here knows much about her or her people. I don't know that she's got any people to speak of, come to think of it. Mind you, I ain't never talked to her – not to pass more than pleasantries, anyway. She and the preacher don't come in here, of course. And I ain't one for church."

"Yeah, what about that? I thought all you country folk were religious."

He puffed on his cigar and said, "I once saw a preacher take a shit before a church service. He was a circuit riding Methodist from Missouri, and I was about seven years old. I was coming through the woods, and he was leaned up against a tree taking a shit. A few minutes later, I saw him get up at a tent revival holding the Bible and talking about Jesus this and Jesus that, but all I could think about was him taking a shit. Been that way ever since."

I stuck my hands in the pockets of my vest and looked out the projector window at the empty theater. Claude had swept it out a little earlier and plugged in a fan.

"Too bad you never talked to Sister Amberly," I said. "You missed out."

Claude peered at me over his cigar.

"You best stay away from her."

I turned around. "What does that mean?"

"Stay away. That husband of hers ain't a man to trifle with."

"I don't know what you're implying, Claude."

"That's good." He measured some film, cut a frame with scissors, and spliced two reels together. Then he started unspooling another reel onto the platter. "Obadiah Henshaw was in the war, you know."

"He told me. Lotta guys were in the war."

Head down, with his cigar just a few inches away from the highly flammable film, Claude spoke through plumes of smoke. "Obadiah was in the Pacific. Got a Medal of Honor for bravery."

"That's impressive. You know what he got the medal for?"

"Sure. Everyone around here knows. Big deal when it happened. During a battle on one of them little islands, one of our boys got captured by some Japs. Japs was dragging this feller away, and Obadiah jumped them. Kilt three of them to rescue this feller. Shot one to death, stabbed one to death, and beat one to death."

"Jesus."

"Yep. So you see what I mean now. He ain't just some hillbilly with his nose buried in the good book. He's a serious customer."

"Was he always that way?"

"Well, let's say he was always a handful. But he weren't always religious, no. He used to be quite the hellraiser in his youth. That changed after he got blinded. Then he became hell's worst enemy."

"How'd he get blinded?"

"Wacked upside the head with a rifle in the war. Fractured his skull. When he come to, he couldn't see nothing."

"Is ... is that how head injuries work? I never heard of that before."

"Heck, I don't know. But when he come back home he was blind as a bat, full of the Holy Ghost, and dragging that pretty wife after him. That's been a year or more now. Don't reckon I ever saw a man change so much. Maybe that Jap rifle rattled his noggin."

I looked through the projector window. A man and woman were in the theater.

"Hey, looks like you have a couple of customers."

I followed Claude downstairs into the lobby. The lights were on and the place looked pretty good. I'd changed the poster outside and stacked some lobby cards by the cash register.

The door to the theater opened, and the man and woman walked out.

The man was as big as an armored car. Except for the bright red scalp visible beneath his blond flattop, his skin had been baked brown by the sun. He smiled when he saw Claude but frowned when he saw me. His big, dull faced turned to the woman for direction.

Next to Amberly Henshaw, she was the prettiest woman I'd seen since Kansas City. Her cheekbones were high and her lips were full and plump. Like the man, she had blond hair and a face that got a lot of sun, but her pale green eyes were the opposite of his. One look at him and you knew he was a big dummy. One look at her and you knew she was sharp.

She smiled. "Evening, Claude."

"Evening, Lucy."

"Opening for business?"

"Gonna try."

"Obadiah Henshaw lift the embargo?"

"Naw, but I figure to run a picture anyways and see if anyone turns out for it."

Claude turned to me. "This here is Billie."

"Billie Dixon," I said, extending my hand.

She gave me a strong handshake and stronger eye contact. "Lucy Harington," she said. Smiling, she added, "The big ox behind me is my brother Eustace."

I extended my hand to the big man, but both Lucy Harington and Claude shook their heads.

Claude said, "Eustace don't much go in for shaking hands."

Eustace stared at his sister, waiting to see what she wanted him to do.

She told me, "He's pleased to know you, though."

Then the big man smiled at me. I smiled back and gave him a little wave.

To Lucy I said, "Well, it's nice to meet you both."

"What do you do, Miss Dixon?" she asked.

"I work for one of the studios that leases films to Claude."

"Oh yes? How're things in Hollywood?"

"Oh, when the smog isn't choking people to death it's pretty sunny."

"You ever meet any movie stars?"

"Sure, I met a couple. Tom Neal tried to pick me up once at a bar. Saw Lizabeth Scott at a nightclub."

"What about Cary Grant? You ever meet him?"

"No, can't say I ever did. He works in a different part of town."

She grinned. "That's too bad. That is one handsome man."

~ ~ ~

Some more folks came in and after a while Claude had a crowd of about twenty people. While the picture played, he sat up in the projectionist's booth. I sat downstairs, just behind Lucy Harington and her brother.

About five minutes into the movie, a drunk man opened the back door of the theater and stumbled in.

"Picture showing? Picture showing?"

Lucy Harrington turned around in her seat and said, "Dave, why don't you have a seat and be quiet now?"

Dave was about fifty and even in the silvery light from the screen I could see that he'd drunk himself to a scarlet hue.

"Okay, okay," he said.

He stumbled to a seat and settled in.

The picture is a crime thriller rip-off of *Hamlet*. A kid whose dad has died has a bizarre dream about his mother and the man she's going to marry. Turns out the mom's new boyfriend is the killer. It's pretty predictable if you know *Hamlet*, but I was pretty sure the Eureka's audience was skimpy on their Shakespeare.

The drunk in the back probably couldn't read – and even sober he probably couldn't have decoded the film's story – but he berated the picture and farted and giggled.

Lucy Harrington leaned over and whispered something to her brother. Then she stood up and walked to the door at the back of the theater.

Eustace stood up, all six foot five inches of him.

He walked up the aisle, took the man under the arms and lifted him out of his seat. The man tried to protest, but Eustace just held him at arms length, like a man carrying a soiled baby, and Lucy opened the door. In a moment they were both out the door.

The rest of the crowd barely noticed. They'd seen Dave drunk before on many occasions, I gathered, and they had not seen a movie in a while.

I, on the other hand, had already seen *Strange Illusion* three times. I hustled out the back.

Eustace had carried Dave to the grass in front of the theater and set him down.

"Why'd you do that?" the drunk demanded.

Lucy stood beside her brother and told Dave, "You go on home now before you get in trouble."

"I didn't not ... did not do nothing to nobody," he said. "Listen here, Sheriff Harington – "

"You get on out of here before Eustace has to bop your ears. You remember what a headache that gave you last time?"

Dave considered that for a moment, turned around, and staggered off without saying another word.

I said, "You're the sheriff?"

I don't know why, but in the same instant, I got scared. My palms started sweating as if I was a criminal with my face on a wanted poster back at the sheriff's office.

Lucy Harington smiled. "No," she said. "Eustace is the sheriff, and I'm his administrative assistant. Which means I get to do all the paperwork."

"But you're the sheriff?"

"Well, let's just say that together we get the job done."

I turned to Eustace. He grinned and nodded.

~ ~ ~

While the Haringtons went back inside to watch the movie, I walked upstairs to the booth. "The sheriff wears a skirt?" I asked.

"She's a lady," he said. "Ladies don't wear britches in Stock's Settlement. They wear skirts. You might remember that."

"I'm wearing a skirt."

"Yeah, but you seem like a woman what owns a pair of trousers. Am I wrong about that?"

"No," I said with a smile.

"Might be best, you keep them in your luggage."

"You got a lady sheriff, though?"

Claude watched the picture through the window. "Well, no, not exactly. Eustace is the sheriff, and Lucy's his administrative assistant."

"Yeah, but – "

"Folks like the Haringtons. Their family's been around these parts forever. The grandfather was mayor during the War Between the States and he kept things on track, so people like the Harington name. And ole Lucy is sharp as a tack, a real shrewd girl. Her daddy made out in the timber boom days and married a educated lady from a nice family down in Osotouy City. Lucy takes after her, I expect. Smart, pretty girl like that – it's a shame she's shaping up to be a spinster. I reckon she's had her hands full with Eustace."

"Yeah, what's the story with him?"

"Well, if dumb was peaches he'd be a cobbler. Strong as a mule, though. Never goes nowhere without it's with Lucy leading him around. Folks around here call him The Strong Arm and her The Law. That's about right. Eustace is gentle as a kitten, but he'd rip off your head if she told him to do it."

"I got that feeling watching him carry the drunk out of the theater."

"Yeah, but Lucy only uses him when she has to. Most times she can talk a feller down. When she does turn Eustace loose, though, look out."

~ ~ ~

When the picture was over, Claude and I went downstairs. The folks filed out, and the Haringtons stopped to say goodnight.

"How'd you like the picture?" I asked.

Lucy Harington smiled. "Well, we missed that part in the middle when we had to drag out ole Dave, so I'm not real sure I caught everything, but something tells me I'd still be confused even if I'd stayed to watch the whole thing."

I laughed. "It's a queer one, but I like it."

"Oh, I liked it, too. Any picture that steals the plot from *Hamlet* has something going for it."

"I'm surprised you caught that."

I must have said it with a little too much genuine astonishment because the lady sheriff replied, "My mother was the English teacher at our school for many years, Miss Dixon. Her great love was Shakespeare. I inherited her love of books along with the books themselves."

"I'm sorry," I said. "I didn't mean to imply anything."

She nodded. "Goodnight Miss Dixon."

I took a step toward her. "Lucy, I want to apologize. What I said was just a reflection of my own rather limited perspective. Please accept my apology. I'd surely hate for us to get off on the wrong foot. And, please, call me Billie."

She smiled, if not warmly, then at least politely. She said, "That's nice of you to say, Billie."

She held out her hand and we shook. She had a farm girl's grip and looked me in the eye. In another reality, I thought, she could have been governor of the state.

The big man was too dense to take note of what had happened. He simply followed his sister out the door. I watched them walk down the street, back toward a little building that sat catty corner from city hall. A little sign on the side of the building read: Law Enforcement.

I said so long to Claude, and I walked down Main Street to my motor lodge. It was late May and warm, but not yet too hot or humid. A full moon illuminated a sky that seemed crowded with stars. I walked through downtown, crossed Appleton Avenue, where Main Street effectively dead-ended at the front door of the American Quality Motor Lodge.

The old man at the front desk raised his eyes from his chessboard just long enough to give me a wave, then returned to planning his next move against himself. The lodge had four rooms lined up in a row, but I appeared to be the only occupant.

I went into my room and sat down on a chair in the corner. I lit a cigarette and sat there smoking, staring out the window at the empty street, thinking a little about Lucy Harington and a lot about Amberly Henshaw, thinking and thinking about tomorrow.

Chapter Five

I woke up the next morning to find out that the world had ended. Or at least the papers implied that things were winding down. I was on my way to wash up in the little bathhouse next to the manager's office, and I heard a couple of old men in front of the lodge worrying over a newspaper.

"Truman Doctrine," a hunchbacked man in overalls said. "That's what they call it. Ole Harry wants us to run around the world shooting it out with the Reds."

The other old-timer leaned back and scratched the liver spots on his bald head. "Don't hardly make no sense. Can't see what bidness we got in Turkey. Sides, how long until that Stalin feller gets his fingers on the bomb?"

His friend considered that. "Ah, them Russians ain't smart enough to figure all that mess out – you know, the science and such."

The bald one said, "I don't know. It's just the way of things. You hit me, I'm a-gonna hit you back. You shoot at me, I'm a-gonna shoot back. And if you get your smart boys to cook up a bomb to blow me up ... you think I ain't a-gonna set my smart boys to working on the same deal?"

The old men stopped talking when they saw me walking by with my towels and toiletries. Almost as one, they said, "Ma'am."

"Morning, gentlemen."

I walked to the little bathhouse and pulled open the creaking door. It was a one room affair with a toilet, tub and sink. One tiny window with a faded curtain faced the woods. I ran the cold clean water in

31

the tub, and when it became apparent that there was no hot water to be had, I dampened a wash cloth and cleaned off that way. Then I washed my hair, dressed, and went back to my room.

The old men were still contemplating the newspaper.

The man in overalls said, "Well, it was foretold in the Book of Revelations that the world would end in fire."

"Did it?"

"You ain't never read Revelations?"

"Attempted it in my youth. Couldn't make no sense of it, so I left it to the preachers."

"Well, the fire's a-coming," the man in overalls said. "You can bet on that. The fire is a-coming."

~ ~ ~

I had breakfast at a greasy spoon on the town square called Dub's Breakfast and Lunch. When I walked in, a waitress with sweptback hair, carrying an armload of plates to a young couple with a baby, said, "Howdy."

"Howdy."

"Anywhere you want."

The few customers in the place looked up and either gave me blank stares or slightly disapproving looks. The young couple with a baby stared at me so long I nodded at them. The man turned back to his wife and raised his eyebrows. She smiled at him.

I sat near the front by the window, and looked down the street at the Sheriff's office. I didn't see any sign of the Haringtons.

The waitress came over. She was probably no older than me, but she had the look of a woman who'd already started lying about her age. She wore more makeup than seemed to be normal for the town, and certainly more than was required for her job – though by the standards I'd seen in certain sections of Hollywood it was pretty tame.

"Morning," she said. "You staying over in the motor lodge?"

"Yes," I said, somewhat surprised by the question. "I'm in town on business."

"You're the movie lady, right?"

"Yes. How'd you know?"

"Oh," she said, "we only got a few hundred folks in the whole of the city limits. Every person that rolls into town becomes the local curiosity for a while. Folks don't mean nothing by it. They're just curious is all. Plus, you being a woman on her own, driving a car, from Hollywood of all places ... Yeah, folks just want to get a look at you." She held out her hand, "I'm Helen."

I shook with her. "I'm Billie," I said.

She smiled. "Yeah, you're a real curiosity, all right."

Helen brought me some expertly fried bacon and eggs, along with coffee strong enough to power a B-17, and I ate and watched life drift by on the street. As people passed Dub's, they all paused to take a look at me. Helen was right, though. There seemed to be no malice in it. I was just the town's new oddity – like a one woman traveling geek show.

I had settled my check and was about to get up from the table when I saw the preacher walk by.

Carrying a Bible in one hand, in the other he swung a long cane rod that looked to have been converted from a fishing pole. He swung it in a wide arc, from side to side, as if driving away rats in his path.

I checked the clock hanging on the wall next to a painting of a bowl of fruit. 11:04.

Amberly said the preacher was going visiting after

lunch. I took that to mean that he would return home for lunch, only to leave again afterwards. Or perhaps he had decided to do his visiting before lunch.

I could feel the beat of my heart, could almost hear it echo through my body.

I stood up and walked outside. The preacher was already far down the sidewalk, sweeping the cane pole before him. I moseyed after him, making as if I was taking an interest in the town square, giving the city hall a good once over.

He turned at a corner. I quickened my pace, got to the corner and made the turn.

The dusty side road led between a hardware store and a shuttered storefront. I walked down the road, passed the buildings, and found myself at some trees and another road leading off toward the river.

But the preacher was gone.

~ ~ ~

I went back to my room at the motor lodge and paced in front of the bed.

11:30.

I made a list of business connections to see on my drive back to California.

11:35.

I checked myself in the mirror. My hair was dark and short – not as short as Bergman in *For Whom The Bell Tolls* but more the finger wave style that been all the rage in the thirties. I'd kept it because it looked good on me. It covered my ears and bobbed just a bit at my cheekbones. My long, thin eyebrows arched over my eyes nicely. I hadn't had a drink in a while so my hazel eyes were uncharacteristically bright. All in all, I looked pretty damn good. For me, anyway.

11:39.

My hands shook.

Are you going to do this? Go see that woman? That woman married to an Arkansas preacher who killed three men?

I sat down on the bed. The creak of the bedsprings stirred something in me. I lay back and stared at the cracked white ceiling. Amberly. I thought about the body that had moved beneath her clothes, the promise that clung to her skin like perfume.

11:43.

I decided I'd wait. I would make myself wait until one o'clock. But I would go.

~ ~ ~

When I got the church, no one was around.

Standing by my car, I called, "Hello" but no one came out.

I walked up the steps and tried the double doors at the front of the church. I don't think they even had a lock. Easily and silently, they opened into the blue sanctuary. Twenty pews divided into two sections faced a raised stage, altar and choir loft, while four stained glass windows seemed to breathe quivering rays of sapphire light into the center aisle.

I walked down the red carpet leading to the altar. Bolted to the back wall was a cross no less than six feet tall and two feet wide. I walked to the back of the room, behind a piano flanking the stage, and opened the door I found there.

It was the preacher's office. Nothing adorned the wooden walls, and behind his bare desk stood skinny bookshelves with only a few scattered, dusty volumes.

The only thing of interest in the office was another door.

I opened it and stepped into a small apartment.

The den was nearly as spare as the office had been, but it showed some signs of a female presence.

On a chair seated in front of an unlit stove, I saw an old issue of Photoplay magazine with a cover photo of Judy Garland leaning against a piano.

The den opened into a small dining room with a single round table and two chairs. A cupboard held some old china and glassware.

I skipped the kitchen and went directly to the bedroom.

It was as spare as the rest of the house. A simple queen-sized bed on a black wrought iron frame. A bureau with no jewelry, no makeup.

But there was a brush. I picked it up and pulled out a long strawberry-blond hair. I wrapped it around my index finger.

Floorboards creaked behind me and I turned and Amberly Henshaw stepped into the doorway.

She looked the way she had before – hair down at her shoulders, a long dress down to her ankles, no shoes. The only difference was that she was not smiling.

"Not much is it?" she asked. "My little home."

"I'm sorry I just came in," I said. "I called outside, but no one answered."

She looked around the room as if she was seeing it for the first time. "You must think this is all so ugly and plain."

I placed the brush back on her bureau. "Not all of it."

She leaned against the door. "The church and this tiny parsonage were already here when we got here. He won't let me dress it up. Too ostentatious, I suppose."

"Too ... ostentatious?"

"Yes."

"I see," I said. I looked at her bare feet, then raised my eyes over her body until I settled on her face. "I'm sorry to hear that. I'm sure you'd make it beautiful."

"You must have seen some beautiful things, living in Hollywood, knowing all those famous people."

I nodded and took a step toward her as a shiver traced my spine like fingertip. "I have seen amazing beauty," I told her. "I've seen hotels made of marble, and swimming pools as big and blue as the sky. I've seen millionaires and movie stars and models, but I've never seen anything as beautiful as the woman in front of me."

She smiled as if I'd just told her I liked her outfit, and said, "Well, aren't you sweet."

I leaned against the doorway and crossed my ankles and slid my hands into the pockets on my skirt. Lowering my chin, I looked up at her.

"Are you glad I came to see you?" I asked.

"Of course. I get so few visitors. Obadiah is a man of single purpose. He's not much for entertaining guests. And he expects his wife to follow his lead."

"And do you follow his lead?"

"Mostly."

"You seem ... I hope you don't mind me saying this, but you seem to be an odd fit for this life."

"It's not what I had planned. That much is certain."

"No?"

She shook her head. "I was the prettiest girl in town in the middle of nowhere," she said. "He was a cute boy in an army uniform on his way to the front. He was good looking and a fast talker. Had a lot of plans for after the war, plans to take me out of Missouri and go out to California. We got married in a passion just before he got shipped out. I sent a lovesick boy off to war, and a month later I found out I was pregnant ... No one around here knows about

37

this. I'm not sure why I'm telling you ... Isn't that strange?"

"It's not so strange. Sometimes it's good to talk to someone who won't judge you."

"You've made no judgments of me?"

"Only good ones."

She said, "I lost the baby. I'd been afraid that I could lose it. My mother lost three babies herself. I wrote to Obadiah to tell him, but by that time he'd already been wounded and lost his sight. The man who read him the Bible also read him my letter. After what he saw over there, and after losing our baby, I think Obadiah just decided there was nothing except God worth seeing anymore."

"So when he came back you followed him here."

"I thought I should. I thought it was the right thing to do. Everyone seemed to think it was the right thing to do. He got the Medal of Honor. I was marrying a hero who wanted to dedicate the rest of his life to God." She looked around her bare home as if she was seeing it through my eyes. "I just didn't know it was going to be like this."

I couldn't think of anything to say to that. I just stared at her.

"Let's go outside," she said.

I fought the impulse to reach for her, to pull her to me. I could still feel the single strand of hair wound tightly around my finger. Somehow, it kept my hand from moving.

She took a step into the den and tilted her head toward the backdoor. I nodded. As I pushed myself off the wall to follow her, she turned and walked through the den.

I had not noticed that my breathing was irregular, but as I followed her I became aware that it was returning to normal. I was starting to cool because I knew this game too well. The empty flirtation that led nowhere. I'd seen it before. Some people like to get right up to the edge of what they desire so that they can feel, however briefly, the heat of its nearness before they back away unsullied by the thing itself.

She opened the backdoor of her home. Three narrow steps led down to a small green field boxed in by trees.

She stood on the second step. I stood on the top step. She reached past me, our chests almost touching, and closed the door. But she didn't pull away as I expected her to. She leaned in, closer to me, her face against my ear. She smelled my hair, and she ran the tip of her finger down my neck.

I raised my hand, the strand of hair unspooling around my finger and falling away as I gently brushed the soft curls from her face.

"Do you want to touch me, Billie?"

"Yes."

"Touch me," she said.

I ran my fingers across her cheek, to her neck. With my left hand, I pulled up her skirt, caressing the smoothness of her thighs. She closed her eyes. I kissed her. Her lips, so soft, kissed me back as if she were tasting something delicious for the first time. This was new for her, I could tell, and the softness and warmth of it sent a shudder through her and she pulled me close, pulled my hand further up her thighs, to her naked clit. Caressing her, I watched her mouth as a moan escaped her lips like a trembling prayer.

"Please don't stop," she whispered.

I didn't.

"Oh God," she said. "Oh God."

I ran my other hand up her shirt, around her back and unclasped her bra. As I fondled her breasts, she pulled up my skirt and slipped her hand down my panties. When she started to caress my clit, my knees almost buckled.

I slid my fingers inside her while I rubbed her with my thumb. She moaned blasphemies in my ear and begged me not to stop.

I didn't.

~ ~ ~

She walked me back to my car, hovering close to my elbow. After we'd collapsed against each other on the back steps of the church, we'd lay there together, entangled in each other's arms, feeling the gasping breaths beneath each rise and fall of our breasts. Now, however, we didn't touch, but we walked in time like we were in a wedding precession. I could still feel her sweat on my face, but I didn't wipe it away. I wanted to feel it dry against my skin.

We walked through the shadow of the church and I had to ask her, "Will he be returning soon?" I wanted to know, but I didn't want to say his name.

"Yes," she said. "He never stays long when he goes to visit. He's not that kind of preacher."

"I don't know what you mean by that. What kind of preacher is he?"

"Well," she said, "I haven't been married to the ministry very long, but I have figured out that if you want to know what kind a preacher a man is you ask yourself what he would be doing if he wasn't a preacher. Some men would be snake oil salesmen, because they're basically just greedy. Other men would be doctors, because at heart they're healers. Others would be college professors, because they're really just frustrated intellectuals."

"What would Obadiah be?"

"A police officer," she said.

"Really?"

"Yes. I think he was drawn to the ministry because

it gave him authority – at least as far as a lot of people around here are concerned it gave him authority."

Walking back into the sunlight, we arrived at my car. "What do you think now?" I asked.

What I meant was, what did she think now of her husband's authority. But she seemed to hear the question in a different way, as a question about us. She said, "I don't know what to think anymore, Billie."

She seemed fragile and unsure of herself now, standing back from me and clutching her elbow as if she'd bumped it on something.

I didn't know what to say. I wanted to leave, to go back to my room and reflect on what had just happened, to remember it in all its quivering glory. For me, reliving experiences were almost as good as having the experiences. I'd gotten a reputation in Los Angeles for loving and leaving– one angry girl had told me I was "a worse dog than any boy who ever picked me up" – but in truth, I wasn't putting notches on a belt. I had no fellows to drink with and brag to. I've always lived alone with my memories of the women I'd known.

Amberly was waiting for some kind of reply, so I told her, "I should probably go now."

Her eyes narrowed and she pulled back. "I see. That's it, then?"

"No, of course not. I want to talk to you more, but you just said he'll be returning soon. I'm afraid of him coming home to find me here."

She glanced at the road, biting her lip. "That's true."

"When can I see you again?"

"What would be a natural place?"

"Maybe the dry goods store, Pickett's."

"Tomorrow?"

"Yes."

"When?"

"I'll go after breakfast."

"So maybe ten o'clock."

"Yes."

I leaned forward to kiss her, but she instinctively pulled back. Then she checked the road again and leaned forward and our lips touched. It sent a shudder through me. I placed a hand on the car to steady myself.

"Tomorrow," she said.

"Yes," I said.

I got in the car and backed out. I drove back to the motor lodge. I collected my things. I got in the car and drove. I could still feel her beneath my fingertips, could still taste her skin on my lips. I could still hear her whispering, "Don't stop."

I didn't stop driving until I was out of Arkansas.

Hollywood Interlude: The Poverty Row Blues

One sunny afternoon, the man at PRC sat me down in his office and said, "We might all be fucked here." He had a cigarette going in the tray on his desk, but he mashed it out and started another. He saw that I was watching him. "My wife thinks these things make me cough too much, so she wants me to only smoke half of each one. Healthier to do it that way she says."

"Don't you just end up smoking twice as many cigarettes?"

He shrugged. "Hell, who knows. She read it in some magazine." He extended the pack of Chesterfields to me. I drew out a cigarette and lit it with the matches on his desk.

His office was next door to the men's room. As he and I smoked at each other, we heard the flush of the commode.

"So we're sold?" I asked.

"Yeah. Some British guy. We're going to be called Eagle-Lion Pictures from now on. They're shifting things around, combining departments."

"That shouldn't affect us, though, should it? I mean, they still need to move pictures, don't they?"

He pressed the palm of his hand to his eyes and I watched the smoke from his cigarette waft into his slicked-back brown hair.

"I don't know, Billie. I don't know. They fired Ray.

You hear that?"

"Jesus. No."

He puffed on his cigarette. "Ray. Henry. The Greenbaum kid. All three. Gone."

I leaned forward, elbows on my knees. "But they haven't said anything about us."

"No. Not yet."

"But they need us. Right? We're not dead weight. I'm out there schlepping the company shit all over the country for them."

He nodded. "Yeah. That's right. Yeah."

"Someone's got to go talk to these people in Missouri and Tennessee." I looked at the burning tip of my cigarette. "And Arkansas."

"That's true."

"So we have nothing to worry about."

He stared out his window at the shadowy wall of the building next door like it was a distant sunset, let out a long sigh and said, "Well, they might bring in their own people. You never know. That might happen. Some fellow in England is sitting in an office right now looking at a sheet of paper. He's going to do some math and draw a line through some names. It's really as simple as that."

I leaned back in my seat.

"So we might all be fucked," I said.

He just stared off into his brick sunset. "That's a distinct possibility, yes."

~ ~ ~

The Moonlight Bar and Lounge was a dim, smoky little joint with two great selling points: it was quiet, and it was located within stumbling distance to my rooms at the Chateau Michel below Franklin. It had a long marble bar up front, and deep dark booths in the back. It wasn't a girl-girl place, but I didn't go there for that. I went there when I just wanted to drink alone, which was not infrequently.

I was sitting in a booth in the back when I saw a group of girls come in. There were three of them. All had the look of studio secretaries still dressed in their work clothes. As they sat down at the bar, a couple of guys who'd been drinking there in complete silence for an hour suddenly got the urge to make small talk, so they slid over to two of the girls. The odd girl out was a short blonde with sturdy legs and a big ass.

I made note of her, but I turned my attention back to the newspaper beneath my half-empty vodka martini. Congress was hunting Commies. At some hearings in Washington the month before, a bunch of people had appeared before a House Committee and warned the whole world about communist subversion in Hollywood. Representing the screen actors guild, guys like Robert Montgomery, Ronald Reagan, and George Murphy had testified that the Reds had been making inroads into the picture business for years. Walt Disney had testified that the Screen Cartoonists Guild was taking orders from Moscow. Even Mickey Mouse wasn't safe anymore. Now a bunch of leftie writers were refusing to testify in front of Congress. The paper said they could all go to jail.

That didn't bother me all that much since I wasn't a Commie, but more problems for the picture business only meant more potential problems for me down the road. I had enough problems already. The meeting that afternoon had given me the willies. Sure, I hadn't gotten the axe yet, but people were getting fired and departments were getting shuffled around. I felt like I was clinging to my job like a heroine hanging off a cliff in one of our shitty westerns.

At the bar, the little blonde with the plump ass excused herself to go to the powder room. She had to pass by my booth to get to the back, though, and when she did she saw me sitting there in slacks and a comfortable shirt and tie. I gave her a smile.

"Bill," she said.

I kept smiling. I knew I knew her, but I did not know her name. It wasn't one of the those deals where the name was on the tip of my tongue, either. I'd just forgotten it completely.

She waited for me to come up with it, and while I smiled and stammered, she said, "Felicia Charbonneua ..."

I said, "I don't know how I could have misplaced a five dollar moniker like that one, Felicia."

Uninvited, she sat down in the booth across from me. "You don't remember me, do you?"

I gestured at the martini in front of me. "I fear that after a few of these, my memory starts getting a little spotty."

Felicia Charbonneua wore a little azure hat atop some swirling pale hair. Under it, she had a round forehead and round cheeks and a round chin – all of which seemed to be held together by a button nose. As she leaned forward, I could see that her eyes were clear and blue. "I'll give you ten dollars if you've had more than one drink, Bill."

She had me there. I'd only had half of the one.

"Maybe it only takes one," I said.

"No, but after two, you get mean."

"What?" I searched my memory for Felicia Charbonneua, but I could not put her together with anyone I knew.

"It's fine," she said. "You forget lots of girls. You and I met at the Well Well Club one night. That was probably '44 ..."

"Oh."

"Oh, yes."

"And did I get mean after two drinks?"

"We had an unfortunate experience, let's just leave it at that."

I gave her a tight smile, but she just stared at me.

"So what do you do when you're not having unfortunate experiences at the Well Well Club, Felicia?"

"Script girl at Republic."

"How're things at Republic?"

"Fine. I heard you were at ... is it still called PRC or did that change?"

"It's Eagle-Lion now. You heard I worked there?"

"It's a small town." She gestured at the newspaper headlines. "You worried about that?"

"About what? The hearings?"

"Yes."

I chuckled. "I'm not a Commie."

"Well, neither am I, but ..."

She let her voice drift off. She seemed to be hinting at something, but I was missing it. "What?" I asked.

She crossed her arms on the marbled tabletop. Her voice lowered. "It just alarms me to think that the government might come poking around the all studios."

"But if you're not a Red ..."

"Our guardians of public probity pretty much equate any degeneracy with being a Red."

"Oh. Yes. But there's enough degeneracy to go around in this town."

She bit at her plump bottom lip. "I know. That's exactly what worries me. Once they start, where are they going to stop? There's enough fuel here for a pretty big fire."

I sipped my drink. "We're small potatoes."

"You're not worried."

"Not about the Committee on Un-American

Activities, no."

She sat back. In a normal tone of voice she said, "Well, you never did worry about much, did you?"

I glanced at her friends at the bar. The men sweet-talking the women, the women allowing themselves to be called "Baby" in exchange for a free drink.

"Are your boyfriends going to miss you?"

She shook her head. "There's only two of them. Mildred and Catherine will keep them busy. Besides, I already have a steady fella."

"He got a name?"

"Harvey."

"What's Harvey do?"

"He's an electrician at Republic."

"You going to marry him?"

She tilted her head. "If he asks me, yes, I think I will."

"Mrs. Harvey ...?"

"Wilson."

"Mrs. Harvey Wilson. That's a real step down, name-wise."

"We have to make sacrifices in this life," she said.

I nodded. "I suppose that's true."

"Except for you."

"What do you mean?"

"You don't strike me as someone who has to make sacrifices."

"You don't know the first thing about me."

Now she smiled, she smiled wide, and the wider she smiled the less she seemed to mean it. "Well, that's where you're wrong, Billie. *All* I know about you is the first thing, which is that you're charming. What I don't know about you is the second thing. I don't even know if there is a second thing."

"This conversation has taken a turn for the worse," I said. "You're starting to hurt my feelings."

She leaned forward. "Do you have feelings, though, Bill? Do you really?"

"Maybe you should go back to your friends and your electrician before we have another unfortunate experience."

"You know, as a matter of fact, I was just on my way to call Harvey," she said. "Let him know that I'm coming over tonight to make him dinner after I have a drink with the girls."

"Give him my love."

"I give him my own. That's enough for him."

"Oh, you *love* him. How sweet."

She shook her head. "I didn't say I love him. I said I *give* him my love. And pretty soon he'll give me a man's paycheck and a home that my parents can be proud of, and after that he'll give me children. Like I said, we make sacrifices in this life. Except you."

"Guess I'm not ready to trade myself in for a garbage disposal and house full of brats in Pasadena."

She smiled sadly, knowingly, like she was talking to a headstrong adolescent. "Oh God, that's what you tell yourself, isn't it? That you have some kind of integrity." She shook her head and pressed the back of her hand to her mouth like she was trying to hold back a laugh. "There were plenty of gals at the Well Well Club, Bill. Why didn't you settle down with anybody? You know why? Because once people get past the charm, they always figure out there's nothing else to you. You're nothing but a needy child."

I leaned over the table and growled, "You were right the first time, Felicia. I don't remember you. That's how important you are – I forgot I even knew you. But you wanted to come over here and insult me so you can feel better about your pathetic life. Fine. I hope you feel better. Now why don't you get your fat ass up and get the fuck away from me before I make a scene in front of your friends."

That shut her up. She liked quietly talking down to me as long as I sat there and took it, but she couldn't afford to have anyone know what we were talking about. She slid out of the booth. "Been nice talking to you, Bill."

She walked to the back of the bar, next to the powder room, and stepped into the phone booth. She put a nickel in the phone and slid the door closed.

I gulped my drink and searched my memory for her. Felicia Charbonneua ...

I remembered the face, but not the name, much less what I'd done to make her hate me. I seemed to remember her eyes, but I couldn't put my finger on the memory itself.

Of course, she was right. To an extent. I'd cut a wide swath through the girls at the Well Well Club when I first got to town. I'd made some friends, too, but in the end neither the relationships nor the friendships had lasted. I don't know why.

I'd seen a few girls pair up – determined, somehow, to make a life together. I wished them luck, but I didn't hold out hope for their success.

I'd seen more like Felicia – the kind who finally sat down and did the hard math on the way things work in this world and decided to settle for some Harvey Wilson who could give them three kids and a house near a supermarket.

And me? Somehow, I'd ended up by myself, nursing my drink and thinking about some pretty preacher's wife more than sixteen hundred miles away.

It had been months since I'd left Arkansas, but I could still taste her mouth on mine. I could still feel her shudder beneath my touch.

I kept going over it, that afternoon we'd spent

together, the way she'd felt and smelled and tasted. But I'd left as quickly as I could. I'd run away, it's true. But I hadn't forgotten her. Forgotten her? Hell, I hadn't stopped thinking about her.

The phone booth slid open, and Felicia walked past me without looking at me.

"Hey," I said.

She stopped and turned around, smiling to herself.

"I didn't forget Amberly."

Her brow furrowed. "Who's Amberly?"

I sipped my drink. "She's the one I didn't forget."

~ ~ ~

After a few more drinks I stumbled home. The air was cool and crisp, but I was in such a foul mood that I actually broke out in a sweat as I staggered down Franklin toward the Chateau Michel.

The place was an eight story apartment-hotel with a front desk that faced the street. Rather than walk around to the front, though, I went in through the big parking area in the basement and took the elevator up to the fifth floor. The hallway was quiet. I had neighbors on either side of my apartment – a miserable-looking couple named the Palmers on the left, and a perky but boring young woman named Kathy on the right. Kathy was the sister of Mr. Palmer and just wanted to live close to her brother, I guess.

I got the sense that Mrs. Palmer didn't like either one of them, but my interactions with all three had been scant so maybe I was wrong.

I unlocked my door and pushed inside. There among the bills and advertisements scattered on my floor in front of the mail slot was a letter from Arkansas.

My breath cut off, and I had to concentrate to get it back. Without even closing the door to my rooms, I ripped open the letter. It was from Claude.

In an almost illegible scrawl it read:

> *Dear Billie -*
>
> *I have asked Jim Nelson to put pen to paper for me to write you this letter. Jim is a feller I know who writes all my correspondence for me.*
>
> *I am writing you to let you know that the preacher has said that he will lift his ban on Motion Pictures. You did it. There is one thing however and that is that he wants to talk to you again the next time you are in our Town. If you talk to him again, he will let me be.*
>
> *Please come back soon as you can and talk to the preacher because he is Adamant. And he is not a man to be put off track.*
>
> *Also when you come back please bring us more pictures with Gale Sherwood. She is real pretty and fellers like to look at her. Eustace Harington sucks his thumb when he watches that BLONDE SAVAGE picture you give us. It has been a big hit especially with Eustace.*
>
> *Kindly Regards,*
> *Claude Jeter*
>
> j/n

I closed the door and walked over to my couch. Sitting down, I lit a cigarette and opened a window. Far down the block, I could see a couple of teenagers rollerskating up the street.

I read the letter again. It said the same thing it had the first time.

I wondered what Amberly had said to her

husband. Surely, she wouldn't have said anything to him about what had happened between the two of us. So why did he want to talk to me?

Did she still want to see me?

I wasn't slated to go back through there for a while. Claude and I had agreed on the next few months worth of pictures – provided he was still in business – and I'd already coordinated deliveries from different theaters in the region.

But I knew I wanted to go back. I wanted to see her. I'd run away from her once, but I did want to go back, to see if maybe ... no, I couldn't even bring myself to think it.

There was no scenario in which Amberly Henshaw got into my car and came back to California with me. There was no way that would work.

I smoked the rest of my cigarettes sitting by my window, looking out at the sky. I thought about Felicia Whatsername's sneer and Amberly's soft mouth. By the time I mashed out the last cigarette, I knew I was going back. If not to get Amberly, then at least to see her again.

I went to bed. I thought about a lot that night. Looking back on it now, though, I realize that I gave almost no thought to the question of why the preacher wanted to talk to me.

Part Two:
The Woman From
Missouri
Fall, 1947

Chapter Six

None of the pictures had Gale Sherwood in them, so Eustace Harington would have to suck his thumb at somebody else. Claude stuck his cigar in his whisker thicket and said, "Why ain't you got no more of her pictures?"

"I don't know," I said. "I guess ol' Gale only made one for us. I got some more crime pictures. *The Big Fix* has Shelia Ryan. She's very pretty. I also have some more Michael Shayne movies."

Franklin Roostervelt walked by and Claude leaned down and scooped him up. Leaning back in his creaky office chair, he smoothed the rooster's feathers. "Gentlest creature I ever met, this damn bird. Never met his equal. Not among the poultry of the world, anyways."

I sat on Claude's desk with my paperwork in my lap. "How'd you come by him?"

"How does one usually come by a rooster?"

"Claude, I have no idea."

"By way of a chicken's ass."

I turned my attention back to my paperwork. "That concludes that conversation."

"You gonna go see the preacher?"

"Yes. Soon as we're done here."

"Oh hell, at this point we're just foolin' around. We already agreed on a whole mess of pictures. The distribution truck will come around every couple of weeks to drop off my orders, right?"

"Yes."

"Then I reckon we're done."

I nodded.

He was right. I was just delaying my trip to see the

preacher. I'd driven over half of the country to see the Henshaws, only to delay myself here.

"Any idea what he wants to see me about?" I asked.

"No, I do not," Claude said petting the rooster.

"He seem mad?"

"He got anything to be mad about?"

"No."

"Then you got nothing to worry about. Probably wants to give you the hard sell on religion. Something tells me you'll be able to withstand the pull. Then again, maybe not. He may save you yet."

I folded up my papers. "I guess I'll just run over there and have a visit with him and Sister Henshaw."

Claude puffed on his cigar and stroked the rooster's neck. "She may not be up for visitors."

That stopped me. "What? What do you mean?"

"I hear tell she's been out of sorts for a while."

"What's that mean?"

"Oh, I don't know. Just what I heard."

"Has she been sick?"

Claude flicked some ashes toward a tin can on the floor. "Don't rightly know, Billie. I just heard that she's been keeping to herself."

"Maybe she could use a visitor."

He scratched his whiskers. "Hell, I don't see as it would do any harm."

~ ~ ~

As the Ozarks settled into autumn, the trees turned a crazy mixture of scarlet and green, auburn and orange, all mashed together like one of those abstract paintings. When I drove up to the church, the building sat dark and gray in the middle of a torrent of color. Although the day was unseasonably warm and pretty, the storm shutters had been locked over the stained-glass windows as if a tornado was expected. I walked up the front steps and tried the double doors.

One door opened. I stepped inside. The church was as dark and humid as a dustbin.

I walked down the aisle. "Hello?" I called. "Anyone around?"

A few pinpricks of light stabbed through the shutters and into the floors. They sliced over my legs as I walked down the aisle.

I went toward the door leading to the parsonage at the back of the church, but when I got to the altar I heard the groan of boards to my left.

I turned and the darkness smashed into my head. I staggered backwards and tripped over my own feet. Hitting the floor, I saw spots of red against the blackness.

Boots clomped against the floors, legs over me, a hand grabbed my hair and jerked my head.

Through gritted teeth, he seethed, "Abomination."

I clawed at his hand, but he slapped my face and my vision exploded again.

"Thou art an abomination."

I balled up, trying to brace myself for another strike, but he moved away in the dark. I heard his boots clomp, heard his heavy breathing.

"Why you come back here?" he asked.

I tried to make him out in the dark, but with my head still spinning I couldn't even see his outline.

"Answer me, girl."

"You ... you asked to see me."

"No. Why are you here? Not to see me. You wanted to see her."

"I don't know what you're talking ab – "

Then he was on me again, yanking at my hair. I struck out, trying to hit him in the balls, but I only punched his knee and jammed my knuckles. He slapped me – two, three, four times.

The son of a bitch was too strong. I curled up.

As soon as I did, though, he moved away again. "Don't tell no lies in this house of the Lord, you abominated whore. You come back here to see her again."

"Yes."

He took a deep breath. "Yes. Yes, you did. But she ain't here. You missed her. Some women of the church come and got her and took her up to Black Tree for the day. She's been waiting to see you ever since you left, but you missed her. She's coming back, though. She's coming back. You still want to see her?"

I covered my head before I said, "No. No, I just want to leave and never come back."

"I'd wager that such is now the case. But I don't want you going nowheres. You can't come to my town and ruin my wife and then slither away like the serpent, leaving me to live here in this ... in this befouled Eden with my fallen Eve."

The red spots had stopped. The darkness, too, seemed to have receded as my eyes adjusted. I could dimly make out his figure, standing by the pew, just a few feet from me.

I didn't say anything. Anything I said could set him off. If he planned to kill me, I'd have to be ready to move quickly. The longer we talked without him slapping me around, the more time I had to recover my vision and my wits.

He said, "I want you to stay here. I want you to see Amberly. Then I want you to punish her for me."

I blinked at him in the darkness.

"What?"

"Book of Romans. 'God give them up unto vile affections: yea, for even their women did change the natural use into that which is against nature.'"

I didn't have anything to say to that.

" 'But we are sure that the judgment of God is against them which commit such sins.' "

I pulled my feet under me, so that I might be able to make a break for the door.

Hearing my feet scrape the floor, he said, "No use in you running. You run, and I'll tell what you did. Ain't no way you could make it out of the state before they got you. Sexual depravity ain't just a sin, you know. It's a crime. And Amberly, she won't stand up for you. I'll guarantee you that. She'll say you held her down and abused her. Abused her with ... what? A hairbrush? Yeah, I'll make sure she says that. A hairbrush. Think on that. No more Hollywood. No job in the picture business. Just your photograph in the paper next to a photograph of a hairbrush, and a long jail term down in Eastgate Penitentiary. If I was a wagering man, I'd wager that them guards down there will take turns trying to hump the depravity out of you. That kind of thing has been known to work before."

My stomach lurched. I knew he wasn't lying, and I knew he wasn't just trying to scare me.

"My wife," he said, his voice seeming to slip away. "My sullied Eve." His voice broke, like he might cry. "I should have known better. Eden can only be lost."

"What ... what do you want me to do?"

His voice came back, clear and strong. "I want you to kill her."

"I ... no ... I can't ..."

"You can. You will. You ruint her. You might as well finish what you started."

"Please, Brother Obadiah – I"

"I am not your brother."

"Yes sir, but – "

"You will do this. You'll come see her tomorrow at noon. I'll be away on a visit. You'll lead Amberly into this sanctuary and you'll kill her right here in front of this altar. I'll arrange for some ladies to come up to the church. They'll find her."

He stood up in the dark. He walked over to me and leaned down. "I'll know if you try to leave town. Everyone will know. And I will sound the alarm. The moment you try to leave is the moment you might as well take your own life."

"But if I do this ... then what? If I kill...your wife. Then what happens to me?"

He stood up. "Then I'll leave you to God almighty. What he has in store for you is worse than any punishment I could deliver."

With that, Obadiah Henshaw shuffled away into the darkness at the back of his church.

Chapter Seven

I lay down on the bed at the motor lodge and nursed my wounds. I dabbed off a little blood from my scalp where the preacher had ripped out some of my hair. Otherwise, the only real damage I had was a throbbing headache.

I lay back on the bed and wished the county wasn't dry. I could have used a drink to settle my mind.

I had no reason to think the preacher was lying when he said that he would shout my sins from the mountaintops.

I had no reason to think the preacher was lying when he said that I would be arrested for sexual violation.

I had no reason to think the preacher was lying when he said that the men who would imprison me would be a pack of self-justified rapists.

Lucy and Eustace Harington ... I didn't think that they would take part in something like that. But you never know about people. Besides, they'd still arrest me. I'd still be in a hillbilly courtroom on a morals charge that was so unspeakable they probably didn't even have a word for it.

The preacher wasn't lying. It would be goodbye Hollywood and goodbye career. It would be time in an Arkansas jail and a record as a sexual deviant. One day inside would be one day too long.

I got up and went to the door and opened it to get some air. Screaming crickets filled the trees behind the lodge, but Main Street itself was dark and quiet.

A man and a woman walked up Appleton Avenue.

I started to shut the door when the woman waved

to me.

I said, "Oh, good evening."

"Evening, Billie," Lucy Harington said. She wore a simple blue dress with a thin brown belt and brown flats. She stopped to talk to me, but she didn't cross the avenue to do it.

Eustace wore blue jeans and a white button up shirt. He looked at his sister.

"The movie lady, remember?" she told him.

He nodded and smiled at me and let out something of a friendly grunt.

"How's the picture business?" Lucy asked.

I nodded as if that was a kind of answer. "Oh," I said, "it's been good. Real good. I heard Eustace liked *Blonde Savage*."

Lucy turned to give her brother a disapproving look. "He liked it a little too much."

Eustace regarded the ground.

Lucy told me, "I'm glad you're back in town, though. Means new entertainment in store for us."

"I suppose so," I said.

"No Cary Grant, though," she said.

"I'm afraid not," I said. "He doesn't do PRC pictures."

Lucy smiled. "That's too bad. He is one handsome man."

"He is."

"Well, we're heading down to Dub's to get a bite of supper."

"I thought Dub only served Breakfast and Lunch. Isn't the name of the place Dub's Breakfast And Lunch?"

"Oh, Dub doesn't even own the place anymore."

"Oh."

"Feller name of Sam owns it now. He serves a dinner. Except on Sundays."

I smiled.

She smiled back. "I guess we got our own way of doing, Billie. I can't claim that it always makes sense, but it has the virtue of being consistent."

We said so long, and Eustace and I exchanged goodbye waves.

I watched them walk down Main Street. I took a pack of Pall Malls from the dresser by the door and shook out a cigarette.

Lucy Harington would be the one I'd have to deal with if something happened to Amberly.

I lit a match and I'd almost lifted it to the butt when a thought stopped my hand.

I had just blithely considered killing Amberly Henshaw.

I dropped the match on the ground and closed the door. Laying back across the bed, I felt a strange unease. It was as if I felt awkward being in the same room as the woman who'd just had that thought. In the room, alone with myself, I felt crowded and uncomfortable.

I couldn't just kill Amberly. *could i* I couldn't just kill anyone. *could i* I'd never be able to live with myself.

Could I?

No.

But if it came down to it. If the choices were narrowed to killing someone or going to jail. Then that was choice I would have to make in my own favor. Who wouldn't?

But Amberly. I couldn't kill her. I'd kissed her, felt her breath on my face, felt her muscles move beneath her skin. I'd been alive with her for a passionate moment in the sun.

I could not kill her. Even to save myself.

But the preacher, was there any reason to let him

live?

He'd beat me. He'd beat her. He was the one threatening to ruin my life.

I lit my cigarette.

The more I thought about it, the more I wondered why he'd ever let me go. Why would he have me kill the woman he loved and then turn the other cheek while I rode out of town? The more I thought about it, the more impossible that seemed.

He wanted me to kill his wife in his church. In front of the altar. While he was visiting some congregant.

I smoked my cigarette. When it was gone, I smoked another. As the smoke drifted up the ceiling, my thoughts cleared and sharpened.

He didn't want her killed. He wanted her murdered, in an obvious way that would warrant an investigation. In a town of a few hundred people, a stranger like me would be an immediate, obvious suspect. At that point, the preacher could tell them any twisted story he wanted.

I couldn't make a run for it. I couldn't let the preacher ruin me. I couldn't kill Amberly.

That left me with one option.

Chapter Eight

It rained the next morning. The warm blue skies from the previous day had been swept aside by gray sheets of cold rain that slapped the top of the motor lodge and plastered autumn leaves to the top of the station wagon.

I stood in the doorway of my room and smoked cigarettes and watched the occasional car splash by.

Obadiah expected me at the church at noon. That meant he would be somewhere else by that time. The way I figured it, he wanted to be wherever he was going *by* noon, so that his whereabouts would be established. He couldn't drive. That meant one of two things. Either he was walking, or someone else was driving him.

I wanted him to walk. But as I watched the rain pound Stock's Settlement, I worried. Would he walk in the rain? A blind man?

I hadn't seen a phone at the church, so I didn't know if he could call someone. He might.

I didn't know. I didn't know much at all. I watched the rain and worried and smoked cigarettes.

~ ~ ~

At ten o'clock, the rain still hadn't let up. I put on a black skirt and white blouse, wrapped myself in a long coat, pulled a forest green kerchief over my hair, and dashed out to the car.

I started it up and backed out of the motor lodge. The usual old man was sitting in his office, staring at his chessboard.

Appleton Avenue curved around the edge of town, so I took it rather than driving down Main Street as I usually did. Gray rain slicked the graveled avenue, but when I got to the dirt road that led toward the church, everything turned to mud.

As I wound up the hill, the sky seemed to be trying to stop me. Wind and rain battered the car. Red sludge spat up at the wheels. I could barely keep the heap on the road.

When I reached the top of the hill, I pulled off into the woods and shut off the car. Through the trees, I could see that the stained glass windows of the Blood-Bought Tabernacle were shuttered, but yellow light shone from the windows of the parsonage in the back. Down the hill, the waters beneath the bridge were high but they had not flooded.

Was Amberly already home? Would she be coming up the hill behind me? Did she have a car? Would she be driving? Would someone else be driving her?

I took out a cigarette, but my hands shook too much from the cold. I fumbled with the matches and finally gave up.

I just sat there.

~ ~ ~

The storm beat on until eleven, when all at once it simply stopped. The front door of the church opened and the preacher walked out. It was as if he'd turned off the rain because it was time for him to leave.

He walked out of the church, swinging his fishing pole. He came down the hill rapidly, like a man wholly unafraid of a misstep. Although he wore all black, by the time he crossed the bridge his pants were red with mud up to his knees.

From where I was parked in the trees, I could see him begin to ascend the hill. The muddy climb slowed him. He used his cane more as a walking stick now, helping to dig in and get sure footing in the sludge. I watched him until he came to a bend in the road obscured by the hill. In a moment, I knew, he would mount the hill not far from where I waited.

I started the car. I floored the gas.

Mud sprayed behind me.

As I ripped around the turn in the road, he tried to jump out of the way.

I swerved to hit him.

He slammed into the front of the car and tumbled over the hood and smashed into the windshield and spun off the roof. I hit the breaks. When I did, the car skidded, the back end whipping around. I fought the wheel, but the car whirled off the road and into a ditch, crashing to a stop in the mud.

~ ~ ~

Cheap motion pictures covered everything. The canisters lay broken in the back of the car, their celluloid contents spilling out the shattered back window and filling the front seat.

I blinked mud and blood and sweat out of my eyes. Glass covered me. The hard film stock had sliced the back of my hand like a paring knife.

Holding my side, I tried to take a breath but my chest ached like someone had punched me in the lungs. I opened the door with my free hand and splashed out into the red muck.

Rivulets of water ran down the hill. Wind shook raindrops from the trees.

I found him on the other side of the road. He'd slid down into a muddy bank of leaves and twigs. A few feet away from him in the trees, the leafy ground plunged further down a rocky black crevice.

He lay broken and bleeding.

I limped down to him.

His front teeth were gone and his right leg was twisted backward below the knee.

He turned his head to me. "Wh-who, who is

there?"

His eyes were open, blank and useless.

"I need ... help," he said.

The shock of the moment rattled my brain. I said, "I'll get help." I didn't think about what I'd done. I didn't think about the fact that he was still alive. For a brief moment, some natural instinct in me took over. For a moment, it was as if we had actually had a terrible accident.

I bent down. I wiped blood from his eyes. "You'll be okay. I'll get help."

He grabbed my bleeding arm. "You? You did this?"

"I came ... I was driving my car–r"

"You did this."

"No ... I was ... driving. I was just – "

He grabbed at his twisted leg with his free hand. "My leg," he moaned. He tried to pull himself up, but when he did his Goddamn leg just fell off. It slid a little further into the mud. Obadiah let out an awful scream.

Breaking free of his grasp, I tumbled backward. As I scrambled to my feet, I glanced, just beyond the trees and the church, distant slashes of blue in the gray sky.

"Please, get help!" he screamed.

I ran up the hill toward the road, but an old fallen tree lay in my way. Sodden black at the stump, its top had long ago been scattered into pieces. I stopped, my blood dripping in thin spots against the damp bark. I turned back to where Obadiah lay fumbling with his belt. I picked up a chunk of the tree about the size of a piece of firewood. Heavy and solid, it fit my hand like a club.

Obadiah pulled his belt out of his hoops and tied it around the bleeding stub that was all that was left of his right leg.

As he did, I lifted the log above my head. He turned to me and I brought it down on his face.

The pictures always get murder wrong. In a picture, one fellow cracks another in the head with something and it's all over. It's like pulling the cord on a lamp.

But Obadiah didn't die when I hit him. The log thumped against his head, one solid object striking another. He screamed and tried to crawl away, but I beat those two solid objects together again and he slowed down. I hit him again, and he stopped.

Chapter Nine

I threw the log down the rocky crevice. It clattered down and disappeared into the dark. I went back to my car, but it was sunk almost sideways into the mud. I climbed back to the road and looked through the trees to the church.

Light still shone from the windows.

Was she there already?

I walked down the hill bloodied, covered in mud and leaves, my hands and chin shaking. Wind seared my face and stung my eyes. My side ached even worse than before.

As I climbed the muddy road toward the church, mud filled my shoes. Mud splattered my muddy legs and caked my muddy dress in yet another layer of mud.

I finally reached the church and went around to the parsonage. I pushed my way in through the backdoor and called her name.

But no one came. I called it again.

She wasn't there.

Panic seized me. I wanted her to take care of me, to tend to me. I wanted to collapse into her arms. But she wasn't there.

What should I do?

Stay there and wait for her? But what if she wasn't alone when she showed up? I'd never seen a car around the church. Someone might be driving her home. What if they stopped up the road when they saw my wrecked car? I wanted to be there when they found Obadiah.

I went to the washroom. As plain as the rest of the place, it nevertheless smelled like Amberly. I washed the long cut on my right hand. It extended diagonally from the knuckle, over the wrist, and few inches down my arm. I wrapped it with a pink towel.

Then, in the mirror over the wash basin, I finally saw the damage to the rest of me. Nicks to my chin, left cheek, and left eyebrow. My left eye was red. Hair disheveled. Mud and blood spotted everything. My blouse. My dress. My belt.

I ran some water to wash the bits of bark and blood and mud off my face, but I stopped myself.

I looked at my belt in the mirror again.

I hurried back to the car.

The gray sky had closed over me. A few drops pelted my face as I rushed down one hill and then trudged up the other. I was almost to the car when I saw a giant man step out of the woods.

"Eustace!" I called.

He stared at me, his dumb face as empty as a dead movie screen. I hurried toward him and I slipped. It was a real slip, but I used it for all it was worth. I started crying like Bette Davis.

Behind Eustace on the road, a car idled with its doors open.

Two women stepped out of the woods.

Lucy Harington.

Amberly.

Amberly looked pale and shaken.

Lucy just watched us both.

~ ~ ~

Hours later, she sat across from me in the examination room at the back of the house of a doctor named Westwood and watched him stitch up the gash on my arm.

The doctor had cleaned and bandaged my arm, and then I'd been allowed to shower in the guest washroom. Doctor Westwood lived with his wife in a nice two story house at the edge of the town square, a short walk from the Eureka Theater. Someone got my suitcase from the motor lodge, and I changed into the most feminine thing I owned, a lime green dress decorated with tiny white petals.

When I came out, the doctor sat me down on a wooden table and gave my arm a shot of Procaine.

Lucy Harington sat across the room in a hardback chair. She wore a white blouse with a black ankle-length skirt, now muddy at the hemline, and even muddier black boots. Her raincoat was folded over the back of another chair and dripped onto the doctor's hardwood floor. Her hair was pinned up and her cheeks still showed red from the cold winds out on the hill.

She said nothing, just watched the doctor prepare his tools.

I asked her, "Is Amberly alright?"

"She's resting at home. Obviously, she's endured quite a shock."

"I feel so awful. That poor woman."

Lucy nodded.

The balding doctor straddled a stool and leaned down to look at my arm. His remaining hair had been swept up from just above the ear and pomaded into five greasy fingers that clawed his pale scalp in desperation. As he squeezed the sides of my cut together and readied his needle, I looked away.

I made a show of avoiding the general direction of the doctor, and thus the sheriff, and stared out the back window at a young oak tree jerking in the wind.

From the other side of the room, Lucy's polite but firm voice asked, "Would you like to tell me more about what happened, Billie?"

Keeping my face to the window, I said, "I don't know what I can say. I was heading to the church – "

"How come you were going out there?"

"Just to pay my respects."

"Awful bad weather for paying respects."

"I know. And I didn't particularly want to do it, but I'm leaving town today. Or, I was. No other time I could do it."

"You were going out to see the preacher or Sister Henshaw?"

"Well, both. I'd met them both."

Lucy said nothing to that. The doctor worked on my arm. I couldn't feel anything, but I winced a little now and then for show.

"Claude mentioned to me the other day," Lucy said, "that the preacher had requested you come see him."

"That's right."

"Went and saw him yesterday, didn't you?"

I wanted to ask her where she'd heard that. I wanted to ask her why she wasn't asking me about the accident. I wanted to ask her why she seemed to have turned cold to me.

I said, "That's right, I did."

"Was Amberly there?"

"No."

"Huh."

Without meaning to, I turned to look at her.

She was staring at me.

"Did you ask after her?"

"Yesterday?"

"Yes."

"I don't ... remember. Maybe I did. I don't remember."

"If you didn't ask after her, how do you know she wasn't there?"

"I guess I must have asked after her."

"Did you tell Obadiah you were coming back

today?"

"I guess I did. Yes."

"Huh."

"What?"

She said, "I wonder why he didn't tell her you were coming by today. You went out there yesterday. She was out of town with some ladies from church. They went up to Black Tree. You told him you were coming back today. I wonder why he didn't tell Amberly. You would have missed her two days in a row."

I winced like the doctor had hurt me, and I looked away. "I really don't know, Lucy. Maybe it slipped his mind. I think, though – I'm a little shaken up, obviously, so it's hard to get my head straight – but I don't think I would have missed her. I just would have stayed and talked to him until she came back."

I turned back to her.

She was looking out the window now, her eyes distant but not dreamy. She looked like she might be doing math in her head.

"I wonder why he was on the road, then," she said.

"What do you mean?"

She turned back to me. "You were coming to visit. He knew that you were coming to visit. But he didn't tell Amberly this morning, and then this afternoon he took off on foot."

"I don't know," I said. "I can't tell you what was on his mind this morning. Maybe he just plain forgot I was coming."

"I reckon that makes sense," she said. "He agree to let old Claude run the picture show unimpeded?"

"He did."

"Tell me what happened this afternoon."

I took a deep breath. To the surprise of all three of us – especially me – as I began to speak my voice broke and tears ran down my face.

"I didn't see him. I just came around the curb and he was there. I swerved to miss him but he jumped right into me."

Lucy stood up and walked over to me and handed me a silk handkerchief embroidered with roses. "I'm sorry, Billie. I know this is hard. Are you alright? Would you like a moment?"

I dabbed at my eyes. "No, thank you."

"He jumped to his right?"

"Yes." I coughed. "Yes."

She returned to her seat.

"Then what? I know it's difficult, but just tell me exactly what happened."

"He hit the car and tumbled over it. I swung the wheel to the ... right, to my right and I went off the road. I think I blacked out. I don't know how long. Maybe I didn't blackout, even, but I lost control of my senses for a moment. I was simply bewildered. Gradually I regained my senses, and I got out and tried to find him."

The doctor stopped working on my arm to listen to the story, but he didn't lift his head. His sad brown eyes just stared up at me over his glasses.

"He was down the other side of the road. He was dead." I started crying again. Not a lot, just a few tears, but they were real. "I tried to help him. I tried to wake him up."

"I don't understand. You knew he was dead, or you thought he was asleep?"

"I ... both. I know that sounds ridiculous, but I was in a daze. I suppose I knew he was dead, but I wanted him to be alive. I tried to wake him up. When I did ... his leg fell out of his pants. I took off his belt." I looked at her. "I took off his belt to tie around his leg to stop the bleeding, but it was too late."

"I wondered about the belt. You say you tied it around his leg?"

"I – Didn't I? I think I did. I know I had the thought to do it. Maybe I started to do it, and then I stopped."

"Maybe you started to do it and then you stopped," she said.

"Yes."

"Then what?"

"Then I saw that he was dead. I didn't know what to do. I was bleeding and confused and simply horrified at what had happened. I thought maybe someone was at the church so I ran there. I found no one there, so I started to go back to town. That's when I came upon your brother. And you and Amberly ... Mrs. Henshaw."

Lucy looked at the rain spitting at the window and twisted her mouth.

The doctor finished with my arm. He patted my hand like I was a child. Then he stood up and walked out of the room. He had not spoken a word to me.

"What happens now, Lucy?" I asked.

She turned to me and crossed her knees. She said, "The folks at the church will bury the preacher. Not sure what Amberly will do. I can't see her staying in town."

"What about ... me?"

"There will be an inquest."

"Am I in trouble?"

"An inquest is routine in circumstances like these."

"It was an accident."

"That's what needs to be established for the inquest. When one human being kills another human being, it's only proper that the community establish exactly what happened."

"Yes. Of course. Do things like this happen often?"

"No." She lifted her eyebrows. "Not often."

"When will the inquest take place? I need ... I have to work. Other customers in other towns are expecting me."

"Well, I need you to stay in town a few days. Inquest will take place tomorrow or the day after. Besides, that car of yours isn't going anywhere."

"Is it still out ... there?"

"I had the boys over at the service station haul it in."

"Which service station?"

"There's only one."

"Owens."

"Yes."

"I've gotten gas there."

"Only place around here to get gas."

"Right."

She moved her lips up into something like a polite smile that said *alright, I suppose that's all.*

"May I leave?" I asked.

She nodded.

We both stood up. Lucy was a little taller than me, and even though I was freshly washed and dressed in clean clothes, while she was muddied and slightly disheveled from the wind and rain, she still managed to look more put together than me.

I extended my hand to her and said, "I am so sorry about what happened."

She gave me a firm handshake. "I'm sure that's true."

Chapter Ten

The day they buried the preacher, the clouds rolled away and the sky beamed cornflower blue. Despite the clear skies, however, the temperature had dropped. Overnight, the earth had turned to iron.

Everyone in town went to the funeral. There had been some talk about waiting until military rites could be arranged, but apparently Obadiah had been explicit in not wanting a military funeral. He didn't want his military honors to take away from the religious meaning of the service – so that put the matter to bed. The service would be held at the church, without any mention of the fact that the man had won the nation's highest military honor.

I rode with Claude. I'd considered not going, but he showed up at my door with his whiskers slicked down and told me to get dressed.

"I don't think anyone would want me to go," I said.

"Naw, you got to go. It's only proper. Especially since – if you'll kindly excuse my language – you kilt the man."

I dressed in the darkest clothes I had and got into Claude's old International. The truck didn't look a day under twenty years old. It had cigar burns in the seat cushions and dusty chicken feathers on the floorboards.

The truck coughed and spat as we climbed the hill. The ground where I'd crashed had frozen solid – as if nature had made a cast of a crime scene. One carload of funeralgoers had stopped to peek at the spot where the preacher had died.

As we passed by, the people stopped and stared.

"People are going to talk about us, Claude."

Claude's whiskers moved upward. Maybe it was a smile, but he didn't say anything.

By the time we arrived, most of the town had crammed into the church. There were so many people there that the wooden casket was pushed against the far wall. Claude and I stood in the back, and word spread that I had arrived. Eventually everyone had turned to take a look at me. Voices fluttered. Some of those voices grumbled.

What can you do with that kind of scrutiny? I tried to look sad, which wasn't difficult.

A pastor stood up to deliver the sermon. He was handsome and young and moved like he owned the place. I was soon to find out that he was Brother Nathan Pickett from the Baptist Church, but that day Brother Nathan seemed to be the only person in the church who didn't have any interest in me. He cleared his throat and everyone turned back around.

"Obadiah Henshaw and I didn't read scripture in exactly the same way," he said by way of introduction. "We had our differences, as everyone here knows. But we knew where we stood with one another. Obadiah always shot you straight. He loved the Lord, and he trusted in the blood and forgiveness of almighty Jesus. And I know he loved and adored his Amberly as much as I love and adore my Rachel." Brother Nathan gestured at Amberly, somewhere on the front row, hidden by the crowd of bodies. "Sister Amberly, everyone here wants to tell you how much they love you. How much they value you. You have the prayers of us all, and you will have the support of us all in the coming days."

Around the church different people said, "Amen. Amen."

"You can rest assured – and we can all rest

assured – that Brother Obadiah is safe in the bosom of his Lord this morning. And I know that he would not have this moment pass without me telling you this morning that Jesus Christ is the risen savior, the forgiver of all sins, the only way to the eternal life that Brother Obadiah began yesterday. We're going to sing Brother Obadiah's favorite hymn, 'Just As I Am' in just a moment. Think on these words this morning, won't you? Ask yourself, if I were to die today, where would I go? What would become of me? We live in an increasingly Godless age, brothers and sisters, but look at what happened to Obadiah Henshaw yesterday. Just like that he was taken from us. So you see, we still need God."

"Amen. Amen."

"We all die. That is the one and only fact we have. At some point, all our todays turn to yesterdays and all our tomorrows get used up. And then, my friends, we're face to face with the Lord of all creation. If you haven't accepted Christ as your personal Lord and savior, what will you say to him this morning? I can tell you what this good man laying here would want you to say. He'd want you to say, 'Yes Lord. Here I come.'"

"Amen. Amen."

"Yes Lord! Here I come!"

"Amen!"

"Let us sing 'Just As I Am' and during this invitation time, if anyone here would like to come up and accept Christ as their savior, let them come up. Please don't put it off, friend. I beg you, don't put it off one more minute."

Together, as one, everyone began to sing. Even Claude knew the words. I was the only one in Stock's Settlement who didn't know the song. It was as if everyone else had been taught the song at birth.

Just as I am, without one plea,
But that thy blood was shed for me,
And that thou bidst me come to thee,
O lamb of God, I come.

Were people looking at me? Was I expected to come to the front, to ask forgiveness for what I'd done? My grandmother hadn't been a regular churchgoer, but I'd been to a few services at the Assembly of God in my youth. I'd seen the people crying up at the front.

The air around me seemed hotter and thicker. As the town sang the song, everyone seemed to be waiting. I couldn't tell if that was normal for the invitation time. Were they waiting on me?

Just as I am and waiting not
To rid my soul of one dark blot,
To thee, whose blood can cleanse each spot,
O lamb of God, I come.

I stepped out. Sweat broke out on my face, and my hands were clammy. I walked down the crowded aisle. The people kept singing as Brother Nathan stepped toward me.

"What's your name, sister?" he said in my ear.

"Uh, Billie."

"What?"

"Billie."

"Would you like to accept Christ, Billie?"

"Uh, yes. Yes sir."

"Do you know that you are a sinner?"

"Yes, I do."

"Do you know that Jesus has died for your sins?"

"Yes, sir."

"Do you want to accept Christ into your heart and follow him in baptism?"

"Uh, yes. Yes sir."

"Do you know that if you accept Christ into your heart, you will have to turn from your sinful ways and walk in his truth?"

"Yes, sir."

"Let's pray. Repeat after me."

He led me through a prayer that basically repeated everything he'd just said. Every so often he'd pause and I'd repeat what he said.

When we were done he turned me around and the song stopped and the whole town stared at me.

With a smile, Brother Nathan said, "Well, brothers and sisters, what we got here is what the papers call a amazing turn of events. I know that Brother Obadiah is dancing in heaven today. Sister Billie has accepted Christ into her heart."

People clapped. People said *Amen Amen*. Some women came to the front and led me to the back room. I was given a white robe. People I didn't know helped me change out of my clothes.

When we came back out some of the men carried in a six-foot horse trough full of water. The preacher told me to stand in it. I did, and the frigid water burned my feet. The preacher asked me to repeat everything about accepting Christ and being forgiven of my sins. I did, and then he plunged me backward into the frigid water.

The cold water scalded me. It shot up my nose. It singed my eyes. It burned every inch of my body.

Then he yanked me out and I yelped and everyone laughed and cried and clapped and said *Amen Amen*.

My skin still aflame, I cried. Through my tears, I saw Amberly for the first time, astonished, on the front row. She wore a dark dress and a black veil, but her eyes were so wide I could clearly see the white around her irises.

I also saw Lucy Harington, staring at me quietly, a few rows back.

And just like that, I was forgiven.

~ ~ ~

Claude lit up a cigar as we drove down the hill from the church.

"Well ... congratulations, I reckon."

My teeth knocked together like dice. I was back in my regular clothes, but my skin and hair were still damp.

"Th-thanks."

"You plan on that?"

"Of course not. I didn't know the man was going to try to convert people at a funeral."

"As good a place as any, I reckon."

My body shook. I had no control over it.

"I have never been as cold as I am at this moment."

We passed by the spot where I had killed the preacher. For a moment, I stopped shivering. I thought about that block of wood I'd thrown down the crevice.

Claude didn't say much until we got back to the motor lodge. Then he parked and puffed his cigar. "Well," he said. "That was one hell of a funeral. Gotta give it that. Preacher Pickett was right, too. Ole Obadiah would have loved it."

I sat there hugging myself, my damp hair plastered to my scalp. "I'm not so sure about that," I said.

"Well, at any rate, it can't hurt you in court tomorrow that you got saved today."

"I guess not."

"Can't hurt that you got saved by a Pickett, either," he said.

"Why would that matter?"

"His older brother Josiah is the prosecuting attorney."

"Oh really?"

"Sure. The Picketts are pretty important around here. The oldest boy is Lionel. He just come back from the war. He runs Pickett Dry Goods. Took it over from old man Pickett."

"Think the prosecuting attorney will go hard on me tomorrow?"

"I ain't no lawyer," Claude said. "Just tell them the truth of the matter. That ought to get the job done."

I thanked him for the ride and got out of the truck. Without saying any more, he gave me a wave and backed out.

I went into my room and wrapped my hair in a towel. I changed into some red pajamas and climbed into bed and pulled the sheets over my head and balled up as tightly as I could. I lay there a long time, letting my body warm the sheets. Gradually, I uncurled and lay there, considering things.

Getting baptized at the man's funeral couldn't hurt my chances at the inquest. Still, I wondered what Amberly thought.

I hadn't heard from Hollywood yet. I'd wired the man at Eagle-Lion right after the accident, but the response had been complete silence. In the meantime, I didn't know if I still had a job. The car would be running in a day or so, but it was banged up. I'd lost a couple of pictures in the wreck. They'd spilled outside the car and had been ruined. And I was days behind schedule getting to other towns.

All in all, it was a pretty bad situation.

And yet, at that moment, the thing that I still kept thinking about was Amberly. Not the man I'd killed. Not the job I might be in danger of losing. Amberly.

"Amberly ..." I said aloud.

Then, as if I'd summoned her, the door opened and Amberly Henshaw walked into the room.

Chapter Eleven

She wasn't alone. Not by a damn sight.

At least ten women – though in the bustle I couldn't take a head count, so there might well have been over a dozen – crowded into my room behind her. No one had knocked. No one had introduced themselves. All of them were still dressed in their church clothes from the funeral. I saw several Bibles.

Amberly said, "Sister Billie, I've come to talk to you."

I sat up in bed, pulling the covers up to my clavicle. "I ... okay."

"I've been talking with the ladies of my church, and when I told them that the Lord has filled my heart with the desire to face you, they convinced me that we should come over here."

"Wh-why?"

She took a labored breath. "I saw what you did this morning, and I want to join everyone else in rejoicing in your salvation. I do. But first, I have to forgive you. I want to truly forgive you. But that, however, will be difficult. You killed my husband. I know it was an accident, but that doesn't change the fact that you took away my husband."

"What ... happens now?"

"I'd like to pray with you. These ladies have agreed to bear witness to this healing. They've agreed to stand in prayerful vigil outside this door as you and I get right with God."

I looked around the room at the horn-rimmed glasses and beehive hairdos of the church ladies. Some of the women looked at me with thinly-veiled disgust. Others looked as warm and welcoming as a spring day. All waited for me to answer.

"I would like to do that," I said. "To get forgiveness, not just from the Lord but from you."

The ladies nodded soberly, and Amberly showed them outside. After just a moment, I heard them begin to sing.

> *Alas, and did my savior bleed*
> *And did my sovereign die.*
> *Would he devote that sacred head*
> *For such a worm as I?*
>
> *At the cross, at the cross*
> *Where I first saw the light*
> *And the burden of my heart rolled away.*
> *It was there by faith I received my sight*
> *And now I am happy all the day.*

Amberly stepped back inside and closed the door, checked that the heavy curtains allowed in no light from outside, and crossed over to the bed. She sat down beside me and kissed me.

She slipped her hand under the sheet.

"Amberly ..." I said.

She shook her head. "No talking. Not yet."

She pulled the top of my pajamas down.

"Amberly don't," I whispered. She touched me. "Don't stop."

She didn't.

~ ~ ~

As the church ladies sang another hymn, Amberly told me, "I know you hit him on purpose."

"I ..."

The word just hung there. She was staring at me, waiting for me to admit it. Not because she had any doubt that she might be wrong, but because she wanted to get past the meaningless denials.

"Yes," I said.

"I can't believe you did that for me," she said.

"No ... I can't either."

"We can be together now."

This time her eyes betrayed doubt. It was a question she was trying to ask me.

"Yes," I said. "We can be together."

"I'll testify for you tomorrow."

I warmed to that idea immediately. "Yes. You can tell them – "

"That you're well and truly repentant for the accident. The whole town will know that the ladies and I came over here to see you after you got baptized. It's all perfect."

"Will anyone ... suspect?"

"Suspect what?"

"About this. About us."

She shook her head. "It's too ... it's so bad, this thing between us, that they don't even have a word for it. It's unspeakable. Unthinkable. If they did suspect, they might lynch us. But it's simply unthinkable to those women. That's one reason I brought them over here. There's no way I could have come alone. Everyone would have known and started to wonder. But now there's a story, and it's a story that everyone wants to believe. That's what I've figured out over the years. People always believe the story that fits what they want to think."

That reminded me of the preacher. I said, "Do you want to know what happened to your husband?"

She leaned back a little and tilted her head. "Did he die immediately?"

"No. He spoke to me. Asked me to get help."

"Oh."

"He knew. When I killed him, Amberly, he knew it was me."

"Why are you telling me this?"

"Because I want you to know."

"But why?"

"I don't know. Maybe I want you to tell me it was the right thing to do."

"That's all anyone wants, isn't it? To find someone to tell them that they're not a bad person. Fine. You did the right thing. You want me to tell you that poor miserable Obadiah was a bastard? He was. He just couldn't see. His blindness didn't make him a gentle soul."

The women outside sang

It is well
With my soul
It is well, It is well
With my soul.

"God, why did you tell him about us?"

"I didn't. He just knew. What I said about people not thinking the unthinkable – that didn't apply to Obadiah. He *only* thought the unthinkable. Remember when I told you he would have been a cop in another life? He would have been. He was always suspicious, always ready to believe the worst about people."

"But why didn't you just deny it?"

"Oh, Billie. That didn't matter. Not at all. Denying it only made him more angry. Now I was a liar *and* a whore *and* a degenerate. He was never inclined to believe a woman, anyway."

Outside, the ladies switched to a new song. They seemed to be flagging in intensity.

"I should go," she said.

"Tomorrow then..."

"Tomorrow, I'll tell the inquest that you and I prayed together and I've forgiven you and that I believe that what happened was a terrible accident."

I stood up. We kissed again.

"I love you," she said.

It was the first time either of us had said it, and hidden away in our dark room while those women outside waited for us, the words took on more power. Something about her scared me now. She'd known all along that I'd killed Obadiah. She'd arranged for this little public show of forgiveness. In the wake of her husband's death, she was moving without any sense of remorse or loss. I'd committed the crime, but she seemed happy to be rid of him, and somehow that frightened me more than what I'd done. Yet, at the exact same time, as we kissed I felt more drawn to her than ever. The fear only added to the excitement. I'd thought I was playing her. Now I thought maybe she was playing me.

I said, "I love you, too." And, in that moment, I really think I meant it.

~ ~ ~

Amberly opened the door and walked outside and told those women that we had prayed and that I had well and truly repented for what had happened.

She turned to me to let me speak. I started to tell the women how deeply I appreciated their prayers and Amberly's forgiveness, but I burst into tears. It was the damnedest thing. I couldn't have planned to cry at a better time. The ladies smiled and dabbed tears away and praised the Lord.

They all came to hug me before they left.

One woman – portly, with a tight steel-gray beehive – held my hand while she told me, "I think this was God's will. That accident was the Lord's way of calling Obadiah home, and it was his way of calling you into repentance for being in the motion picture business."

"I think you're right," I told her. "I think you have something there."

She nodded and let go of my hand.

Amberly gave me a sisterly hug, and then she took the arm of the lady with the steel-gray beehive and they walked back to a waiting car. I watched the caravan of five vehicles drive away.

From the front porch of the manager's office the old man had left his chessboard and stared at me.

I stuck my hands in the air. "I've been saved!"

Chapter Twelve

The next day, the inquest was held on the top floor of the city hall in what looked to be the only courtroom in the building. The judge was a tall man with unruly ashy-blond hair who took off his glasses at the beginning of the proceedings and spent the rest of the morning cleaning them with the end of his tie.

Legal representation was assigned to me by the court. I was told that I wasn't on trial, but that I was entitled to legal assistance if I felt it necessary. The court appointed lawyer was a tiny old man with thick glasses and an even thicker stink of old sweat and penny cigars. He wore a filthy suit with a shirt that had long since aged from white to yellow. Before the inquest began, he did not say a single word to me.

The judge didn't say much. Most of the talking was done by the prosecuting attorney, Josiah Pickett. Unlike his handsome younger brother, Josiah was an obese man squeezed into a tight white suit. He had a spherical body with a spherical head, and as the heaters in the room clanked and hissed, he took out a handkerchief and dabbed sweat. He looked like a melting snowman.

The first witness he questioned was Lucy Harington.

Josiah Pickett said, "Court will note that Sheriff Harington could not be here today and in his stead, his administrative assistant, Miss Lucille Harington will be offering evidence for the sheriff's office."

I turned around and looked at Eustace sitting on the front row, smiling as his sister took the stand.

After the preliminaries were out of the way, Pickett asked, "Miss Harington, could you describe the incident that took place on November 17th?"

Lucy wore a smart brown dress with a white hat and heels. "Yes sir. The sheriff and I were giving Mrs. Amberly Henshaw a ride out to the church – "

"If I may interrupt, Miss Harington, a ride from where?"

"The sheriff and I were in town when we saw Mrs. Henshaw downtown. She was picking up some groceries at Pickett's. She was with a lady from her church, Mrs. Aloysius Hermann. The ladies had been out delivering supplies to some elderly shut-in members of their church. They had not anticipated the rain so soon that morning. Because Mrs. Hermann lives out on Baxter mountain, she wanted to get going back home in case the storm got worse, so Eustace and I – the sheriff and I – offered to give Mrs. Henshaw a lift out to the church."

"Please continue."

"We came out to the top of the hill just before you cross the creek to the church and we saw a car had run off the road. We stopped and looked into the car but we couldn't find the driver. We looked around and on the other side of the road we found Mr. Henshaw."

"That was Obadiah Henshaw, the pastor at the Blood-Bought Tabernacle and husband to Amberly Henshaw."

"Yes sir, that is correct."

"What condition was he in?"

"He was dead."

"Could you describe the condition of his body in a little detail for the record, Miss Harington?"

"Yes sir. He'd clearly been struck by the wrecked car. He was bloodied in several points – his face, his neck, his hands. And his right leg had come off at the knee and lay a few feet from him. A portion of his scalp, perhaps the size of a dollar bill had ripped off."

"I apologize for asking a lady to describe such a scene, Miss Harington."

"That's quite all right, sir."

"Was it your impression at the time that the deceased had been struck and kilt by the car?"

"Yes sir."

"Are you today of the same opinion?"

"Yes sir."

"What happened next?"

"As we were looking at the body, Mrs. Henshaw became upset. As she was crying, the sheriff went out to the road. Coming up the road from the church was the driver of the car, Miss William Dixon."

"For the record, Miss Dixon has a man's name?"

"Yes sir. The name on her California driver's license reads William Dixon. She goes by Billie."

"Miss Dixon is here today?"

Lucy turned to me and pointed. "Yes. She is sitting at the defense table next to Mr. Oglesby."

"What was her condition?"

"She was bleeding at her arm. She had cuts on her face. She was dirty from the mud."

"What seemed to be her state of mind?"

"She appeared to be very upset. She fell down and cried."

"What did she say happened?"

"That she had come around the bend in the road and struck Mr. Henshaw as he was walking."

"Did she appear to be drunk?"

"No sir."

"Did the sheriff's office find any evidence to suggest that she was drinking or was in any other way impaired as she was driving?"

"No sir."

"Did the sheriff's office find any evidence of malice or intent?"

"No sir."

"I think that will be all, your honor."

Without looking up from cleaning his glasses, the judge said, "Don't forget to ask about Eustace."

"Oh yes. As the sheriff's representative here today, do you know of any further information that the sheriff's office would like to enter in to this proceeding?"

Lucy straightened up in her chair and said, "Yes sir. One thing. It seemed to me that Miss Dixon did not have a plausible explanation for why she was going out to the church that day."

"Oh? What explanation did she give you?"

"That she was going out to pay her respects to the preacher."

"Why does that strike the sheriff's office as implausible?"

The sheriff's office thought about that a moment. "Miss Dixon is only an occasional visitor to our town. She's only been here twice. To the best of my knowledge, she did not know Mr. or Mrs. Henshaw very well. The day in question, the weather was very bad. Stormy. An odd day, I thought, to go visiting someone you don't know very well."

"I see. But, to be clear, you still believe that the death of Mr. Henshaw was an accident."

"Yes sir. I just thought I should mention that there was still a question that needed answering."

"Thank you, Miss Harington."

I was called to the stand next. After swearing me in, Josiah Pickett asked, "Miss Dixon, can you tell us what happened?"

I repeated the story I had told Lucy, almost word for word.

The judge cleaned his glasses. The sweaty snowman wiped his face. Mr. Oglesby sat at his table and stunk.

Lucy sat next to her brother and listened. As was always the case, I couldn't read what she was thinking.

Pickett asked, "To address the question raised by the sheriff's office, why were you going out to the church on such a rainy day?"

"Mr. Henshaw and I had become acquainted on my last visit. He had opposed motion pictures, and we had talked through some of his concerns."

"How did you do that, exactly?"

"I reassured him that the motion picture company I work for makes good wholesome films of an uplifting and entertaining nature."

"And you were going out to see him ..."

"Just to pay my respects. I was due to leave town the next day. I wanted to thank him again for lifting his ban against motion pictures. It seemed like good business to me to see him one last time and make sure he was happy."

The court thanked me and called up Amberly.

She came dressed in black. As she took the stand something about her came into focus for the first time. I'd always known it without being able to put my finger in it. She always looked completely at ease. I'd never seen her in any context in which she seemed upset or confused. She always looked calm.

"Mrs. Henshaw can you tell the court what you saw the afternoon of the 17th?"

"Yes sir. As Miss Harington said, she and the sheriff offered to give me a ride out to the church. As we came up the hill we saw the car off the side of the road. We stopped and got out, fearing someone might be hurt. We found ... my husband."

She held a tissue to her mouth.

"The court will keep this brief, Mrs. Henshaw. When you and the Haringtons found your husband, what condition was he in?"

"He was dead."

"And then you saw Miss Dixon?"

"Yes. She came up the hill. She looked awful. She collapsed."

"To the best of your knowledge, ma'am, was there any bad feelings between your husband and Miss Dixon?"

"No sir. She and my husband had talked about the pictures she was selling to the Eureka Theater. My husband was not a fan of motion pictures, as everyone knows, but she had convinced him that she had a good heart and her pictures were of a good moral quality, if not of a particularly high artistic quality."

Everyone in the court snickered at that.

She smiled sadly. "I rather think Obadiah liked Miss Dixon. She had spirit, he said. He admired spirit in a person."

"Do you have any other pertinent information you would like to given this court?"

"Yes sir. Just one thing. Miss Dixon came to the Blood-Bought Tabernacle yesterday and received Jesus Christ as her personal Lord and savior. Afterwards, she and I had the opportunity to pray together. I want to tell the court that in my opinion, what happened out on that road the other day was a terrible accident that this woman feels deeply sorry for. More than anyone else, I would want to punish someone for the death of my husband. But what happened was, I believe, an accident devoid of intent, malice, or negligence. I feel she has paid enough for it – in terms of guilt and sorrow. I want this court to know that, speaking on behalf of many of the ladies of my church, I believe that the Lord has used this accident to bring a lost soul to Christ. I know that my husband is in heaven right now, rejoicing that his death brought one last soul to the Lord."

The judge smiled at his tie and glasses and made no comment about the theological implications of me running over Obadiah. The prosecuting attorney thanked Amberly for her testimony and excused her.

Lastly, Josiah Pickett called up Dr. Westwood, the same silent doctor who had patched me up. He apparently also worked as the town coroner. Pickett asked the doctor what had killed Obadiah Henshaw. The doctor turned out to have a voice as country as bowl of okra. He sounded more like a moonshiner than a doctor.

"He got struck by a car. He had glass in his head, chest and hips. He had several broke bones. His leg had been knocked off at the knee."

"Based on your examination, what kilt him?"

"Trauma to the head. Looked to me like when he got threw clear of the car he hit some trees going down the hill. Whacked one pretty good with his face."

Josiah Pickett thanked the doctor for his testimony.

"I think that's all, your honor."

The judge put on his glasses.

"All right, then," the judge said. "I don't think we'll need a recess. This court finds that the death of Mr. Obadiah Henshaw was an accident. The combination of rainy weather and bad driving conditions, together with the fact that the deceased was blind and the driver was a woman, produced a terrible situation that was all but unavoidable. The court extends its condolences to Mrs. Henshaw and thanks her for her moving testimony here today, as well as her fine example of Christian charity. As for you, Miss Dixon, good luck to you. In the future you might try to avoid driving in the rain."

With that he banged his gavel and left the room.

My legal representative, Mr. Oglesby, who had not uttered a single word in court that day, congratulated me and presented me with a bill for twenty-five dollars.

Amberly came over and shook my hand. "God be with you, Miss Dixon."

I left the court alone.

~ ~ ~

When I got back to the motor lodge, the old man at the front desk waved me over and handed me a Western Union telegram. It was from the man at Eagle-Lion. It read:

> Billie Dixon
> Stock's Settlement Ark Nov 21 1947
>
> Received your message regarding wreck. You are instructed to return as soon as able. No need to make further calls on customers. Return with car account books and all salvageable company stock.

I carried it to my room and sat down on the bed and read it again. I didn't have to read it a third time. Twice was enough to get the main point.

I was out of a job.

Chapter Thirteen

The world turned white overnight. I woke up to find ice and snow covering the town. It wasn't deep. It was more like a thin white gauze had been thrown over everything in sight.

I dressed and walked down to Dub's for breakfast.

Helen waved me to a seat by the window.

"How you doing this morning, sweetie?"

"Cold," I said.

She carried over a pot of coffee and poured me a cup. "So ... congratulations on getting saved."

"You heard about that?"

"Heard about it – sweetie, I was there. I sang along while they dumped you in that horse trough. Guess that makes you Baptist, now."

"Or a horse."

"Well either way, it's better than being a Methodist. What can I get you?"

"Some toast and eggs."

"How you want them eggs?"

I looked across the street and saw Lucy and Eustace come out of the sheriff's office and start toward the diner. My hands moistened.

"Sweetie, how you want them eggs? Better tell me or Sam will just follow his instincts and fry 'em like bacon."

"Have him do that. Fry them up."

The Haringtons came in and Lucy saw me and smiled. She pulled at Eustace's arm and he followed her over to my table.

"Morning," she said.

"Morning."

"Care if we join you?"

"That'd be lovely."

They sat down. Eustace smiled at me.

"Good to see you, Eustace."

Lucy leaned back from the table and crossed her legs.

"He's glad to see you, too. He likes you, you know."

"Well, I like him."

"I suppose I should congratulate you."

"On what?"

"You've had a busy week. Getting saved, getting cleared at the inquest. Heard you got forgiven by Sister Henshaw and the ladies from the church. All in all, that's a lot to contend with. To say nothing of running over poor Obadiah Henshaw."

Helen came to the table and took the breakfast order for Eustace and Lucy. They both got bacon, eggs, and oatmeal.

I said, "We don't know each other very well, Lucy, but you sound almost sarcastic."

Lucy Harington lifted her eyebrows. "My mother said that a person's tone of voice was the sound of their hidden thoughts."

"Your mother sounds like quite a woman."

"She was quite a woman."

Eustace stood up and walked out of the diner.

Lucy watched him go.

I asked, "Where's he going?"

"He doesn't like it when I talk about Mother. He'll collect himself and come back."

Helen brought over a cup of coffee for Lucy. "I forget, Lucy, you take any short sweetening?"

"No, thank you. Just black."

Helen left and Lucy turned her attention back to me.

"At any rate, you made it through the inquest,"

she said.

"Yes. Thank you for your testimony."

She tapped her coffee cup with her fingernail. "I only told them what I saw, what I thought."

"Yes." I sipped my coffee. "Well, thank you, anyway."

"How are you holding up?"

"I don't know. I'm still unsettled, I suppose."

"That's only natural."

I said, "You know it was an accident, don't you, Lucy?"

"If I knew of evidence to the contrary, I would have presented it to the court."

"That's a rather cold answer to my question."

"It's a cold job that I've been tasked with, Billie. I'm neither Sherlock Holmes nor Dolly of the Dailies. I'm just someone trying to do her job. I attempt to do it with a certain degree of precision."

"You told the court that you found ... how did you put it? You found my explanation for why I was on the road to be 'implausible.' I have to tell you, that seems almost insulting. And given that the weight of that hearing, I was very worried when you said it."

Lucy sipped some of her coffee. Then she placed the cup back in her saucer and smiled politely in a way that declined the invitation to comment further.

I said, "Well, I'm just glad it's over."

"And now you're born again."

I couldn't help but smile. "Yes."

She grinned back.

I said, "You know what? At the time, it seemed like the thing to do. I figured it couldn't hurt to square my account with the Lord of the recently deceased."

She nodded. "And now what? Back to Hollywood?"

"Yes. I'll try to look up Cary Grant for you."

"Thank you. Your company must be concerned to hear that you were in an accident."

"Yes ... they were. But I've let them know that I'm alright."

"What about the damage to the car and the films?"

"What about it?"

"The company isn't upset about that?"

"Oh, well, yes. But these things happen sometimes. I'm not the first person to get in a wreck."

"No," she said, staring at my eyes like she was trying to read something illegible.

I shook my head. "You know," I said, "I don't know what it is, but for some reason I can't shake the feeling that you don't quite believe me. And the mystery is, I don't know why I care. I know what happened. The court knows what happened. But I can tell that you have some kind of lingering doubt and it bothers me."

She leaned over the table and said, "When Eustace and I saw Amberly and Mrs. Hermann together at the store, I offered to give her a ride home because old Mrs. Hermann wanted to get back home before the rain. But I also gave Amberly a ride home because I was curious about the old bruises I saw on her neck."

"I wasn't aware of any bruises on her. I didn't see any, but, of course, I was pretty shaken up when I saw her that afternoon."

"She had them. It looked as if she'd been choked."

"Did you ask her about them?"

"No. Of course not. One doesn't pry into someone else's marriage."

"What does that have to do with me?"

Lucy sat back in her chair. "Nothing. Not a thing. It's a simple sequence of events. You arrived in town and met the Henshaws. Then you left town. Then you came back. Then I saw Amberly with bruises. And then you killed her husband with a car."

"I don't know what you're getting at, Lucy."

"I'm not getting at anything. Except maybe this: some part of the story is missing. Something has been left out of the sequence events. I know that."

"Well, if you figure it out, let me know. For now, it sounds like you're putting a bunch of coincidences together and trying make them make sense. I don't know why the preacher might have beat up his wife. Maybe he liked it. Maybe she hit him with a frying pan. I don't know. All I know is I went out to see him to make sure he wasn't going to give Claude any more trouble about the pictures, and I turned the corner and hit the poor guy."

Eustace walked back in the diner and sat down with us.

Helen came over with our food. "Just in time, Eustace."

The big man smiled.

As we ate, I steered the conversation toward safer subjects like the weather and my job. I didn't reveal that I'd been fired. I told stories – some true, some made up – about the places I'd gone and the people I'd met. I talked and talked, talked to fill the space between us, but the whole time I knew that Lucy Harington was across the table, thinking.

Chapter Fourteen

As soon as breakfast was over, I excused myself and hurried over to the garage where my car had been towed.

The mechanic was a wiry little fellow without his front teeth. Grease spotted his work clothes and caked his hands and the creases webbing his neck. He leaned against the big doorway of the car bay and masticated a bulge of tobacco in his left cheek.

I asked, "How's my car?"

His lips peeled back so he could spit brown juice through the gap in his teeth.

"Goter done."

"You do?"

He lifted his eyebrows in affirmation.

"How much do I owe you?"

He reached in his pocket and pulled out a greasy piece of paper.

I felt my spirits lift. Then I read the bill. $248. My spirits lowered.

"That's more than I thought it would be. I could have bought another car for that."

He spit.

I had just a little over three hundred dollars. And I no longer had a job.

"I just ... I didn't think it would be that much."

He didn't respond to that, so I just stared at him pleadingly, beseechingly, pathetically.

After a while, he turned and spat into the snow.

~ ~ ~

I drove back to the motor lodge and collected my things. After paying my bill at the front office, I only had $57.17 left in my pocket. That wasn't much, but with a car that ran I could get the hell away from Stock's Settlement. I did not intend to delay my departure.

I carried my stuff out to the car and started it up. For a moment, I thought about dropping by to see Claude. In an odd way, I thought of him as the only friend I had in town.

I decided against it, though. Claude would do fine without seeing me, and I didn't want to risk running into Lucy Harington again.

I backed out of the lodge and drove through town. Through the window of the diner I saw Helen laughing with Sam. I saw the light through the window of the sheriff's office.

I was out on Appleton Avenue before I remembered Amberly.

Should I go get her? Did she really want to leave with me? What would people say? How long would it take anyone to figure out that we'd left town together? Once they knew, what would Lucy say? What would she do?

Being in the car, feeling the ground pass beneath the wheels, I knew I could just keep going. Amberly would be crushed. That hurt to think about, but she wouldn't be the first woman I'd hurt. People hurt each other. She'd get over it. She was beautiful and smart. She didn't have to stay in this town if she didn't want to, and if she couldn't figure that out on her own then she was a fool. Either way it wasn't my fault.

But as I approached the turn for Church Hill Road something pulled me toward her. If I'm honest the pull didn't have all that much to do with Amberly herself.

I was scared. I was alone and broke and without prospects. All I had to do was turn and get her and she'd be with me. I wouldn't be alone.

I turned.

~ ~ ~

As I pulled up, Amberly walked through the snow around the side of the church.

She wore a brown coat over a white blouse and a black skirt. Her hair was pinned up, and she wore a pair of heavy black boots.

I got out of the car and said, "We have to go."

"Go? Now?"

"If you want to leave with me, now is the time. I need to get out of this town."

"Has something happened?"

"I had a talk with Lucy Harington this morning."

"What'd you say? What'd she say?"

"She's suspicious."

"Of us? If she's suspicious, why didn't she say anything yesterday?"

"Look we don't have time for this – "

She stepped back. A large snowflake fell against her pink cheek and she wiped it away. "Please take a breath and slow down, Billie. You just drove up, jumped out of the car and told me that we have to beat a hasty retreat. That doesn't make me want to get into a car with you."

"I thought you wanted to leave with me."

"I do. But I didn't think it would be this morning, on a moment's notice, with some vague warnings about the sheriff's suspicions."

I took the deep breath she'd recommended. I said, "No one is after us. I'm sorry if I seemed panicked. Everything is fine. For now."

"What about Lucy?"

"She and I talked at Dub's this morning. She doesn't like me. But it's not ... What you said before was right, if she had any serious suspicions she would have made them known to the court. She as much as told me that herself. She feels like there's some part of the preacher's death that is unaccounted for – and obviously there is – but that's it. The court cleared me, and I'm free to go. Which is what I want to do. I want to get out of town and out of the state as quickly as I can. The longer I stay here the worse it all gets for me. That much I know. I need to leave, and I want you to come with me. Right now."

She put her hands on her hips and looked up the frozen road. It occurred to me that she was looking up there near the spot where I'd killed her husband, but I'm not sure that it occurred to her. I think she was just staring off, considering her options.

She looked at the house.

She looked at me.

She nodded.

~ ~ ~

It took her ten minutes to pack. She had two suitcases that she filled with dresses and blouses and skirts and shoes. She had an overnight bag she filled with toiletries and a long nightshirt.

She left her Bible. She took her movie magazine.

We should have left at night. There would be fewer people to see us together, fewer people to get suspicious.

But all we knew is that we wanted to leave as soon as possible. She navigated me down the icy back roads she judged least likely to be occupied, and we bumped along in single minded purpose. Neither of us felt any excitement or thrill as we made our escape that day. It was not a lark we were on. Without discussing it, we both knew that if we were caught, the truth, or something like it, would come out – and one of us would go to jail for it.

We twisted and slipped along the back roads until we hit the highway. We'd managed to circumnavigate the town without seeing anyone, and Amberly had guided us to a point outside the city limits.

We hit the highway and headed north. Neither of us spoke. I certainly didn't feel any relief yet. We could still be seen. These hills were peppered with people, and in an area with such a small population, we'd have to drive miles before we found someone who didn't know Amberly.

Yet the wind was at our backs. As we climbed those torturous, snowy mountain paths, the car moved fine and I handled it with the precision of a Hollywood stunt driver. Next to me, Amberly stayed quiet except to give the occasional direction or warn me about an upcoming curve or dip in the road.

I was so focused on the drive that I couldn't afford the presence of mind to really regard our situation. We hardly knew each other. In fact, I knew practically nothing about her. Her age. Her maiden name. Where she was from. Where she wanted to go. Despite having had sex with her and covered up a murder with her, I had only the vaguest notion of who she was. Looking back on it now, that seems incredible. At the time, though, all I knew is that she and I were together and that we had the same goal: to get out of Arkansas.

An hour north of town, we saw some people. A man and a woman and a couple of children were walking down the road. The man, in front, wore a beard and overalls. The woman wore a coat over a garment made of scraps. The child behind the woman was wearing a coat and scraps as well. The child at the end – a girl of perhaps four or five – wore a short coat under which she appeared to be completely naked.

We passed them and all of them glared at us.

After we'd rounded the bend, I asked, "Did you know them?"

"No."

We drove a little further. I asked, "Was that child naked?"

"I think so."

"Christ."

We passed though a town called Baxter a little further up the highway.

"I might stop here."

"Don't," she said.

"I have to use the ladies room."

"I know people here. Brother Walker's church is here. Don't stop. We'll pull over to the road outside of town."

We zipped through Baxter, past a large red church on a hill, past a few houses with smoking chimneys, past an assortment of old cars and horses and mules surrounding an auction house.

Outside of Baxter, I pulled over and we took turns urinating in the woods while the other one stayed with the car.

Then we were back on the road. Neither of us had thought to bring any food, and I started to get hungry around two o'clock, but we didn't stop.

We didn't talk. We just sat there, side by side, staring at the road in front of us, willing it to be behind us.

Finally I saw the sign for the state line.

Next to me, Amberly cleared her throat. I looked over and she was crying.

As we crossed over, I said, "You're free."

"We're free," she said.

Chapter Fifteen

That night we stopped for dinner somewhere in Oklahoma at a roadside joint called The OK Café. Either the place had once been an Indian trading post or the owners had built it to look that way. A hitching post ran along the front of the building, and to get inside we had to push through some swinging doors flanked by wooden barrels.

A pretty girl in a getup that made her look like Dale Evans greeted us as we came in. She tipped her hat at us. "Howdy, ladies. How are y'all today?"

We were both too exhausted to give much back to the girl, but Amberly smiled and said, "We're fine."

"Just the two of you?"

"Yes, please."

She grabbed a couple of menus and showed us past some rowdy families and moon-eyed couples to a booth in the back. We slid in and the waitress left us to the menus.

Amberly looked it over. "I'm not sure I can eat."

"I can."

She gave me a weary grin.

I put the menu down on the tabletop and ran my hands through my hair. "We should stop in the next town we see that has a motor lodge. No idea when that will be."

"We could use the rest. You could use it. You look tired."

I smiled. "Thanks. You're saying I look rough?"

"No. Not at all. Just tired."

"Well, I am tired. I've never had to beat it out of town before."

Looking over her menu she said, "Mm. You did

last time."

"What? What do you mean?"

She glanced up at me. "Last time you left Stock's Settlement, you left in a hurry." She turned her attention back to her menu. "I was pretty hurt, I must say." I stared at her while she turned the menu over. She said, "I think I'll have The Westerner sandwich with a side of cowboy beans. I wonder what cowboy beans are."

The waitress walked over. "What can I do you ladies for?"

"What are cowboy beans?" Amberly asked.

The waitress glanced over her shoulder to see that she was out of earshot of the boss. "Baked beans," she admitted. "Got a bit of bacon fat in there to liven it up. But basically you're looking at baked beans."

"Fine then. I'll take the Westerner and some cowboy beans."

"To drink?"

"A Coca-Cola."

The waitress said, "And for you, ma'am?"

"Black coffee and a ham sandwich."

The waitress thanked us and took our menus. Amberly said, "I need to use the powder room."

She slid out of the booth and I watched her walk to the soda counter and ask a boy in buckskins where the shithouse was.

He pointed her down a hallway.

I stared at the hallway until she came back and sat down across from me again.

I said, "What do you mean?"

"What? About what?"

"What do you mean when you say I left town in a hurry last time?"

With a quiet smile, Amberly looked around the restaurant, at the children running around one table, at a young man and a young woman holding hands across a couple of greasy, empty plates.

She turned back to me. "Right after you and I ... spoke at my house, you returned to your room and collected your things and left town. Heard you didn't even say goodbye to Claude."

"Where'd you hear that?"

She leaned back and the smile fell away. Her eyes searched my face. "It's the nature of the place, Billie. You were quite literally the only stranger in town. When the only stranger in town leaves, everyone knows. Everyone knew you left that night. Right now, everyone knows you left town this morning. There is every good chance that everyone knows I left with you."

"But no one saw us leave."

The waitress brought over our food. When she left, Amberly said, "Maybe they did and maybe they didn't. But if just one person came up to the church to say hello today and didn't find me there, then with you leaving town ..."

"People will talk."

"In all likelihood, they're talking already."

I spooned some sugar into my coffee as she tried her beans. "Oh my. The OK Café has mastered the art of cowboy beans."

"Were you mad when I left town in a hurry last time?"

"I was hurt."

"I know. You said that. But were you also mad? I can only imagine that you didn't look kindly on me leaving you like that."

"I didn't run and put your name on the top of the prayer list."

"But were you mad?"

She dabbed at the corner of her mouth with a

napkin. "I suppose I was, Billie. Don't you think I had every right to be?"

I muttered something in the affirmative and tried my food. The OK Café had not mastered the art of the ham sandwich.

"Why are you asking about that day?" she asked.

I chewed my food slowly. After I swallowed, I took a sip of coffee. She watched me the whole time, waiting for an answer. "I don't know," I said. "You just mentioned that day. Made me wonder if you got mad at me."

"I was hurt. I suppose I was mad. Is there any other reason you have for asking me?"

"No."

She nodded, and we turned our attention to our food.

After a few moments of eating in silence, I asked, "Is there really a list?"

"What do you mean?"

"A prayer list at church."

"There is. People would announce things they wanted us to pray for during the week. I'd write it down. During the week I'd read the list to Obadiah and he'd pray over each name."

"What kinds of things were on the list?"

"Oh, many things. Florabel Stoker always wanted us to pray for her husband Vern."

"What was wrong with Vern Stoker that couldn't be fixed by having a wife named Florabel?"

"He's a drunk. We prayed for quite a few drunks, on pretty much a weekly basis."

"Did it ever work?"

"Opinions differ."

"But what do you think?"

"About prayer?"

"I don't know. About God, I guess. Did you believe

what ... he preached?" I didn't say the preacher's name. For some reason, I couldn't bring myself to say it.

She put down her fork and sipped some Coca-Cola. "If I did, I wouldn't be sitting here with you."

"What do you think about the whole God business, then? Up until a few days ago it was your whole life, wasn't it?"

Her hands opened as if to catch raindrops as she tried to formulate the words. "I don't know what to say about it. I guess everything comes down to people in the end. Some folks are just full of kindness. It doesn't come from anywhere, it's just in them. Other people are full of meanness. And that meanness doesn't come from anywhere, either. Praying to God is just praying that the best in people will win out. That's my thinking."

I had nothing to add to that, so this time when we turned back to our food I let the silence stand. I just watched Amberly. It was odd to see her here, in a diner in another town, in another state. She seemed different – though I couldn't put my finger on exactly how. As I watched her chew her food, I had the oddest realization: I'd never seen her eat before. We'd covered up the murder of her husband, and we'd driven away together to chase some vague dream of happiness together, but I'd never seen her eat.

As she sat there and chewed her food across from me, I was repelled by her. It didn't happen slowly or in stages. I simply watched the rotation of her smooth jaw and I felt a revulsion at the gross animal quality of her body. It was nothing she did. She ate, as they say, like a perfect lady. But she wasn't a perfect lady. She was an animal chewing some food that she'd convert into a shit she'd take somewhere down the road.

Strange, the thoughts that come to you,

sometimes.

"What are you thinking, Billie?"

"What?"

She was looking at me.

"What are you thinking?"

"Just ... how happy I am to be with you. I can't believe you're here."

She smiled. "Me too. It's like a fairytale."

~ ~ ~

We didn't find a motor lodge that night. We drove for hours. It seemed as if the world had turned off. The sky went dark. No stars, no moon. Even the snow gradually all disappeared. The world was dark and the air was sharp and cold.

I stayed behind the wheel. I suppose I was too scared to stop, really. Scared that we'd pull over and a police officer would pull up and say, "Are you those two women who ran away from Arkansas this morning?"

So I kept driving. Somewhere in the night, however, I started nodding off and Amberly shook me. "Billie, we have to stop."

"Nowhere to stop."

"Just pull off the road and we'll sleep for a few hours. Then we can get going again and I'll drive."

I wanted to argue, but I wanted to sleep more.

We were on two-lane blacktop, so we looked for dirt roads off to the side that didn't seem to lead to any house. They were difficult to find, because the headlights of the car only reached a few feet into the dark and we'd see a road only as we were passing it.

After we sped past a dusty break in the trees, I slowed down. "Turning around," I said.

I made a U-turn off the road and back to the spot I'd seen. It wasn't a road or a trail, just a natural divot in the tree line about thirty or forty feet back from the road. I backed into it and pointed the front of the car toward the road.

Amberly pulled a blanket out of the back and covered us. I kissed her and she kissed me back, but she stopped me when I slid my hand up her skirt. "We're not far enough back in the woods for that," she said.

"You want me to find another place to park?"

"If you want to do that, then yes."

"Are you scared?"

"Aren't you?"

I allowed that she was making good sense. Then I debated whether to start up the car and drive down the road until we found something more secluded. I'd only been thinking about it a minute or two when I realized that Amberly was asleep.

~ ~ ~

Over breakfast, she asked, "Are you mad at me this morning?"

"No. Why?"

"Because you've barely spoken a word to me. I thought maybe you were the kind of person who's a little grumpy before they get their coffee, but now you've had yours and you still haven't spoken more than five words to me."

We were in another roadside diner. This one, as near as I could tell, was simply called Diner. That's what the sign out front said, and it's all the menu said.

I lit a cigarette. "You fell asleep last night. Do you recall that?"

"No."

"You don't?"

"No. I just – you should know this about me if we're going to be together – I just pass out when I go to sleep. It's just like" she snapped her fingers "that. Did it hurt your feelings?"

"No. Well, a little perhaps." I lowered my voice, "I thought we were going to ..."

She lifted her eyebrows. "Oh. Mm. Yes, I'm sorry, Billie. Like I said, I'm like an electric light. I just switch off."

"I could take that personally, you know."

"I know, but you shouldn't. I was simply exhausted. It was a very tiring day."

"That's true," I allowed. I shrugged. "I was asleep within a few minutes myself."

"Good. You needed the rest more than I since you drove all day. Today, however, I insist that you let me do some of the driving." She reached over and patted my hand, an innocent gesture to anyone who might see it but one that sent an electric shock through my body when she said, "And we'll make sure we stop someplace with a comfortable bed."

We stared at each other over the breakfast plates.

"Maybe we should get on the road then," I said. "I want to get to that comfortable bed as soon as possible."

~ ~ ~

We were on Route 66 somewhere outside of Amarillo when Amberly said, "I can't wait to get to Hollywood."

While she drove, I'd been sitting in the passenger side with my shoes off, staring out the window at the flat brown Texas earth rolling buy, smoking cigarettes and thinking about nothing in particular. Now I turned to her and said, "Oh, yeah?"

She drove with both hands on the wheel, sitting up straight. "I've never been there. Seen photographs in the magazines, and I've seen it in the movies. But I've never been there."

"I thought you didn't go to the movies."

"Well, not after I married Obadiah, of course, but

I used to go quite often when I was a girl. I just loved Myrna Loy and William Powell. My mother took me."

"I never heard you mention your mother."

"No, I suppose you haven't. She was a very beautiful woman and quite a lady. She died in 1936, far too young."

"I'm sorry to hear that."

She nodded. "It was a terrible loss, one I've never recovered from." Amberly clutched the wheel, whitening her knuckles. "My father, however, recovered quite quickly. He remarried within a year to a woman I detested and who detested me. She drove a wedge between us – though in fairness we had never been close. Father had always wanted a boy and was disappointed when my mother could only give him a single daughter. When this imposter took my mother's place she bore him a son within the year. After that, Father had no use for me. I wanted to attend college, but he wouldn't hear of it. So I did the only thing else I could think to do. I got married. His name was Edward Vincent Penn. A nice man, quite a bit older than me; he owned a store. We were married a few years, good years. He died in 1943. Sitting at our kitchen table, reading in the paper about the battle of the Kasserine Pass. Remember, in Africa? He was sitting at the table reading me something about it, and I was in the kitchen and he stopped in the middle of a sentence. I walked in and he was dead at the kitchen table. When I buried him, it turned out we had no money. I was destitute. I met Obadiah a few weeks later." She relaxed her hands and her knuckles softened into pink again. "Now here I am, going to Hollywood with Billie Dixon."

"I'd say you saved the best for last."

"Tell me about it, about Hollywood."

"It's sunny. It's a place that basically sells

sunshine. Everyone is good-looking."

"Really?"

"Well," I laughed. "No, not really. I'm exaggerating, but only slightly. It's a place where the world sends all its pretty people."

"That sounds delightful."

God, it wasn't delightful at all. Maybe I should have told her the whole truth, which was that it's a factory town that mass produces pictures of youth and beauty, so pretty young girls go out there chasing a dream and they end up getting turned into commodities. If they're lucky, they actually get to be in a movie or two, and then maybe they break out and then maybe they become Joan Crawford, but most just get passed around between the studio men like some kind of perk. Every lower tier executive and hack comedian in town who fancies himself a ladies man can basically buy, bribe, or steal his share of aspiring actress pussy. The casting couch is where dreams go to die, but what's a girl gonna do except hit her knees or go back to Arkansas? No pretty young thing ever showed up in Hollywood just praying she was going to wind up with Bob Hope's dick in her mouth, but more than a few have suffered that fate.

"You know," Amberly was saying, "mother always said I was pretty enough to be in the pictures."

I smiled at that and turned back to the passing land in time to see a hawk swoop down into a ditch. It happened so quickly, the hawk must have killed something. A rat, maybe, or a gopher.

"You said so, too," Amberly added.

"I said what?"

"That I was pretty enough to be in the movies."

"Yes. That's right."

As she drove, she never turned her head to look at me, but just then she glanced at me. "You weren't just saying that, were you, Billie?"

As it happened, I couldn't recall saying those words exactly, but they sounded like a line I might use. I was from Hollywood, after all, and telling girls they were pretty enough to be in the pictures was a line as old as the pictures themselves. "Of course not," I said. "You're a lovely woman, Amberly Henshaw."

"Mm, we'll have to fix that Henshaw bit, I suppose. My maiden name was Fleming. Do you think Amberly Fleming sounds like a movie star?"

"Like a movie star?"

"Yes." Now she turned her head and looked at me. She only looked at me a moment before she remembered herself and turned her attention back to the road, but in that moment I saw something on her face I had never seen before. Innocence. She thought we were going back to Hollywood and she was going to be a movie star.

"Yes," I said. "Amberly Fleming sounds like a good name for an actress.

Her brow furrowed. She chewed her lip. "Good," she said.

~ ~ ~

Before we got to the New Mexico state line, we pulled over at a filling station to get gas and use the ladies room.

As I waited for Amberly to come out, I stood at the edge of the lot and stared out at the scrubby desert. As far as I could see, all there was to see was dirt and rock and scrub bushes. My beautiful native state.

Amberly walked up behind me, and I nodded at the scenery. "I'm always nervous to be in Texas," I said. "It's like I'm afraid of running into someone I've tried to avoid."

"Things will be better once we get to Hollywood."

"Yes."

I turned around. The wind tousled her hair, but her face seemed tight. "Whenever I mention Hollywood," she said, "you get quiet."

"I suppose so."

"Why is that?"

"There's something I need to tell you."

She crossed her arms and chewed her lips.

"I lost my job."

"You lost your job with the movie studio."

"Yes."

"What does that mean? You ... Can you get it back?"

"I don't think so."

"You knew this yesterday. Why didn't you tell me this yesterday?"

"I don't know. I was scared."

"But how am I going to ..." She trailed off, turning away as if to watch the words drift across the cool barren desert. Or maybe she just preferred the rocks to my face. I watched her walk out among the rocks and dry underbrush.

Behind me, the fellow working at the station lounged in the doorway and stared at us. He was rawboned and young with buzzed brown hair and a dimpled chin. He was far enough away that he probably couldn't hear what we said, but he didn't seem to think anything of openly watching us for his amusement. Men did that, stared at you as if you were there to be stared at.

I picked up a pebble and threw it at him. Startled, he glared at me, but he retreated into the station.

When I turned around, Amberly was walking back to me.

"Let's go," she said. "You drive."

We got it the car. She didn't say anything as Texas slipped by. We'd be in New Mexico soon. Sometime tonight we'd stop there, but I didn't think we'd get the comfortable night we had hoped for just a few hours before.

Chapter Sixteen

We stopped for the night outside the town of Brittle Rock, New Mexico at the Days And Nights Motor Lodge. The place had clearly been around for a while, but from the road the bungalows looked like they might be spacious and clean. Out front, anchored by a thick cement base, was a twenty foot sign with a smiling neon yellow sun and a snoozing neon blue moon.

Amberly sat in the car while I went inside to register our stay.

The manager's office was a freestanding pueblo-style building with red clay walls and a tall cactus standing out front like a sentry. As I pushed inside, a bell jingled on the door. From a cracked door behind the front desk, a little voice called out, "Just a minute."

"Okay," I said.

Presently, a little woman shuffled out. She wore glasses, her hair up in a bun. In her left hand she held a dime paperback with her finger marking her page.

"Evening," I said.

"Good evening," she said, taking out the registry with her free hand. "I suspect you'd like a room."

"Yes, please."

"How many beds?"

"Two, please." We only needed one, but it was best to keep up appearances, especially on the road.

"Luggage?"

"Some. We can get it."

"I can get Delmer in here. He's in the backroom napping. Won't take but a second."

"We can get it. We're traveling rather light. No

need to wake him."

"How long will you be staying?"

"Just tonight."

She nodded and passed the registry to me with her free hand. "Five dollars even," she said.

As I signed and paid her, I asked, "Is there somewhere to get breakfast?"

She gave me a room key marked **Bungalow C**. "Brittle Rock café is open at six-thirty. Just down the road a piece. Serves a breakfast."

I thanked her, and she gave me a little wave with the book, her finger still marking her page. I walked outside. Leaning against the car and staring down Route 66, Amberly was smoking one of my cigarettes.

"You don't smoke," I said.

Without taking her eyes off the road, she said, "And yet here I am, smoking. Must be quite a sight." She placed the cigarette in the corner of her mouth and then drew out a white silk scarf from the car.

I watched her tie the scarf around her neck, knotting it tight, and when I was sure she had nothing else to say to me, I collected our luggage and carried it to Bungalow C.

I set down the bags on the little stone stoop and unlocked the door. Leaving the door open, I carried the bags inside.

After a moment, Amberly appeared in the doorway and said, "We need some alcohol."

I turned around and looked at her without saying anything.

"What?" she asked.

"Nothing."

"Good," she said. "Let's get a bottle then."

"I don't know where to go."

"Would the front office have one?"

"I doubt it. She's just an old woman."

"Then maybe in town."

I rubbed the back of my neck and groused, "Amberly…"

"What?"

"Do we have to? We just got off the road. Jesus, we've been driving all day for two days straight. The town's a couple of miles away. The thought of getting back in the car just now …"

She nodded and walked in and shut the door.

The bungalow had wooden floors and red-clay walls. A little sitting room with a desk and a couple of chairs led into a small dining area and a kitchenette. The bedroom and bath were in the back, but they seemed unreachable at the moment.

Amberly sat down on the desk and lit another cigarette.

"Are you mad at me?" I asked.

"Why? Should I be?"

"Maybe a little."

"Why?"

"I didn't tell you about losing my job."

She stared at the cigarette smoke curling to the ceiling. "No, I guess you didn't."

"So, tell me, are you mad?"

She would not look at me. After watching the smoke dissipate against the ceiling she turned her attention to her nails. "I suppose I'm not, Billie. I'm just disappointed."

"Well, I'm not too happy about being out of a job."

"I'm disappointed you didn't think more of me than to tell me."

Footsteps clomped across the stoop and knuckles rapped on the door.

Amberly stood up and came and stood beside me.

I moved to the door and, without opening it, said, "Yes?"

A young male voice announced, "Delmer from the front office."

I told Amberly, "It's okay" and opened the door.

A skinny young man with red ears smiled back at me. When he saw Amberly, he smiled even wider and his ears got even redder. "Evening ladies. I thought I should come check on you. Sorry the old lady didn't wake me when you all checked in. Say ... she didn't tell me we had a couple of movie stars staying with us. Let me see" he balled up his big lips and shot me with his forefinger "you're Ella Raines, ain't you? And you, miss," he said shooting Amberly "why you must be Paulette Goddard. I'd know you anywhere."

I was too tired to fake being charmed, but I managed a weak smile. "Thanks for checking on us, I don't think – "

"Oh, it's no bother for me to check on you. Fact is, I only got the old lady to talk to in there, and once she gets locked into one of her books there ain't no dragging her out of it 'til she's finished."

"Fine. I don't think we need anything now except some sleep."

Amberly said, "Hold on just a moment." She walked over to us and leaned against the doorway. "What's your name, again?"

He hitched up his pants. "Name's Delmer, pretty lady."

"Delmer what?"

"Delmer Q. Duggans, ma'am."

"Delmer Q. Duggans, what on earth does the Q in your name stand for?"

"Quayle. My momma's maiden name. All my brothers and me got Quayle for our middle names."

Amberly said, "You don't mean to tell me that there are more strapping young Duggans boys like you out there."

"Five of us, ma'am. Donald, David, Dick, Darrell, and Delmer."

I butted in, "And the war didn't manage to pick off any of you?"

"Nope," he said. "We all come through in one piece."

"See," I told Amberly, "there must be a God." I glared at her. *What the hell is this?*

"Delmer," Amberly said, ignoring me, "I do think there is something you might do for us."

"Anything at all, ma'am."

"My friend and I – by the way this is Miss Billie Dixon and I'm Miss Amberly Fleming – well, we would like a drink."

Delmer lifted his big stupid eyebrows and smiled his big stupid smile. "Ah, like to do a little drinking before you call it a night?"

"That's right. Do you have access to any booze, here or in town?"

He leaned against the door. "Matter of fact, I do have a bottle for sale. Now, there might have to be a bit of a mark up, being as it's a specialty item and all."

"You run and go get it. And we insist that you have a drink with us."

Delmer just about pissed his pants as he nodded and ran off to get the bottle.

When he was gone, I said, "You asked that moron to have a drink just to spite me."

"Not at all," she said. "I could use a drink and so could you. Makes sense to have one with him. Makes him less suspicious."

"There's nothing for him to be suspicious of, Amberly. We're just two friends traveling together."

She crushed out her cigarette and lit another. "I think I could really grow to like smoking."

"Fine," I said. "Let's just not keep him here very

long."

"Why?" she said. "It's not as if you have something in Hollywood to rush back to."

My face flushed. I heard Delmer running back to toward us, and I didn't want him to see me upset, so I went back to the washroom.

~ ~ ~

When I came out some minutes later, they were drinking and laughing.

Amberly was sitting in a chair with her legs crossed and Delmer was standing next to her, leaning against the desk.

"There she is," Amberly said.

I tried to smile. "What are you two laughing about?"

"Delmer was just telling me the funniest story about the folks who pass through here. Delmer," she said gently slapping the back of his hand, "you really ought to send that to the *Saturday Evening Post*."

"They have the *Saturday Evening Post* in Arkansas?" I asked her. "I'm surprised you've heard of it."

She had a sip of Delmer's hooch and smiled as if I'd said something cute. "Oh, I've been around more than you think."

Delmer looked at her and then at me and then at Amberly again. His ears were scarlet.

"Why don't you pour me a little of that, Delmer?" I said. "And tell me the story, if you don't mind. I could use a good laugh."

Delmer picked up the bottle – a plain brown bottle with no label – and poured me half a glass.

I took it and had a sip. It stung my mouth like a bee. "They still have Prohibition out here?" I said. "This tastes like it was mixed in the bathtub."

Delmer only grinned at that before he eased into

his story. "I was just telling Miss Amberly here about a couple of folks we had come through a few years ago. Newlyweds. Arrived one day on foot, covered in road dust and soaked with sweat. Their car had crapped out on them – if you'll pardon the expression – and they were on foot for miles. Make matters worse, they were already lost when the car died. Don't know how they ended up out here, but that lady, she was fit to be tied. Her husband, he probably wasn't too happy about the situation either, but then on top of everything he had to listen to her bellyaching about it.

"So they stayed here that night. The Nances, that was their name. Mr. and Mrs. Something Nance. They fought the whole night. We heard them. I was younger then, but I stayed up all night just to listen to them cuss each other. You never heard two people talk like that to one another. A woman, too. Never heard such language come out of a woman. Cussed worse than a drunk cowboy.

"That goes on all night. And I mean ... all ... night. The two of them just ranting and raving at each other. Then about four o'clock in the morning, they quit. We figure they've finally tuckered themselves out. About ten minutes go by ... and they commence to, ah, making up. You know, in the way only a man and woman can."

"Sure," I said.

"And they go at their lovemaking just as loud as they'd pursued their arguments. I was shocked, and the old lady was scandalized. And she's seen and heard some things in her time, let me tell you. It sounded like ... well, I don't even know. You know how love scenes are depicted in them romance books? You're ladies, you know what I mean."

"Romance books," I said. "I can't get enough of that stuff."

"Well, this was like that brung to life. Pretty steamy stuff."

Amberly asked me, "Isn't that delightful?"

"Yes. Though I'm not really sure that the *Saturday Evening Post* is ready for it."

Delmer finished off his drink, and before he could reach for the bottle, I said, "Well, Delmer, it's been good to share this drink with you."

"Think nothing of it. In fac – "

"But we have to get up in the morning, so we should probably bid you good night."

Amberly smiled ever so pleasantly at her drink. "Don't you think Delmer should stick around? Maybe we could tell him a story of our own."

"Well, sure," Delmer said. "I'd lo – "

"No," I said. "We need to hit the hay."

"But Billie, sweetheart, shouldn't we tell Delmer all about how we became such good friends?"

I glared at her, but at that moment I felt more fear than anger. "Be careful, Amberly."

Delmer, puzzled, stared at me with his mouth open. "What?"

"It's all so ... boring," I told him. "I don't want you to be bored."

"Not at all," Amberly said. "Delmer, I used to be married. It wasn't a great marriage, but it was a marriage. I lived in a little town up in the Ozarks. Billie here works for a movie studio. Can you believe it?"

"No fooling?" Delmer said.

I shrugged, too nervous now to speak.

"She came to town, and she and I just became the best of friends. Then, one day, she ran over my husband."

"Jesus, Amberly," I said.

Delmer's slack mouth pulled itself into a brief

attempt at a smile and then fell limp again.

"Killed him dead," Amberly said, taking a drink. "And now, to make it up to me, she's taking me to Hollywood. Going to introduce me around. I've got my heart set on meeting Franchot Tone. Maybe I'll be a movie star. Leastways, that's what Billie here says."

Although Amberly had told the story, Delmer asked me the question. "Now, are you pulling my leg?"

I shrugged again. "It's the least I can do for her," I said.

"You know, I want to be honest here," Delmer said. "I took a peek in the back of your car there and I seen them movie canisters piled up. I wondered if you were in the picture business."

I didn't know what else to do, so I just shrugged again.

Amberly yawned.

Delmer looked like he was going to make another try for the bottle, so I said, "Well, with that, Delmer, I think we'll pack it in for the night."

He looked at Amberly for a lifeline, but she finally relented. She'd had her fun, and now she was bored with him.

"Yes," she said. "I guess it's time to say goodnight."

Chapter Seventeen

"**W**hat the hell was that?" I asked after I'd listened to Delmer walk back across the courtyard.

Amberly poured us both another drink.

"Well?" I said.

"Drink that," she said.

"Are you going to talk to me?"

"Are you going to drink that?"

I downed it in one disgusting gulp.

"Well," she said. "That's impressive. It's a skill I didn't know you had. There's so much about you that I don't know."

She stood up and walked across the room. Her skirt clung to her hips as she walked. The booze in my head made it hard for me to focus my thoughts, but I could concentrate on her hips without much effort.

She leaned against the smooth red wall and regarded me over her glass.

"I'm sorry I didn't tell you I was fired," I said.

"Why?"

"Why what?"

"Why are you sorry so on and so forth ..."

I poured another drink. I sipped at it. Delmer's rotgut got better the more you imbibed, but I had to concentrate to get my words out in the correct order. "I'm sorry I didn't tell you. I should have told you."

"*Why* didn't you tell me?"

"I don't know. I suppose I was scared."

"Scared of what?"

"Scared you wouldn't come with me."

"Mm hmm," she murmured into her glass. "And why is that?"

"Amberly are you trying to get me to admit something? I don't know what it is. Is there something I can say ... to ease your mind?"

"You don't believe in me, do you?"

"What the hell are you talking about?" I asked. I felt my face flush. For a moment I tried to arrange my thoughts – to remain calm and think about what I wanted to say and the best way to say it – but instead I just closed my eyes as my orderly mind scattered like the pieces of paper in a gust of wind.

She said, "You don't believe in me, that I could ... really be a movie star."

"What?"

"You said I could."

"I never said ... Did I say ... I don't think I ever said that."

"So it's true. You don't think I could?"

"Oh for Christ's sake, what are you a child? A little girl? You want to be a movie star? You know how many people want to be stars in Los Angeles? Exactly all of them. You know how many will make it? Nearly none. It's, what do you call that ... statistics. You know what statistics is, are? It means almost nobody makes it."

Amberly stared at me, a frigid smile quivering on her lips. "I see. Well, you don't know what I'm capable of. I sat in a dark house in the deep woods with a religious fanatic for over a year and I waited for a bus to pull into town. I waited, and I waited. I choked down my pride like medicine everyday because I knew. I knew all I needed was a train out of town, and you were that train. I can do – "

"That's all I am to you," I shouted. "A train. That's right. You don't care about me at all. You couldn't wait to tell Delmer that I didn't mean nothing to you but a ride out of town."

"Maybe if you believed in me it would be different," she said. "Maybe I'll just get another ride to Hollywood."

I laughed at her, boozy and mean. "Here's what you, what you don't understand. You're pretty for Arkansas, Amberly. You understand? You're pretty for *Arkansas*. You're not a movie star. That's not going to happen. You're going to go to Hollywood without me? Are you serious? You know what happens to girls like you in Hollywood? They get chopped up. They found one dead a few months ago. Some sick bastard raped her, carved her up, and cut her in half. Yeah. Sawed her in half at the waist and dumped the pieces in an empty lot. That's what Hollywood does to the hometown beauty queen who thinks she's going to be a movie star."

Amberly glared at me. "You're ghoulish."

She stalked past me and slammed down her drink on the table. She opened the door and walked outside. At first, it looked as if she might walk toward the office, but instead she veered off. I followed her, out of the courtyard and into the desert.

Everything was cold rock covered in pale blue moonlight. My head hurt already. I was going to have a headache in the morning.

"Where the hell do you think you're going?" I called out to her.

She just kept walking and didn't say anything. Where was she going? There was nothing here except uneven rock and clumps of cacti and brush.

She kept walking, so far ahead of me now that I could see nothing but her blackened figure and the moonlit scarf snapping like a flag in the wind. Did she want me to follow her? Did she want me to catch her and turn her around? How far would we go? How far had we come?

I stopped and turned around. The motor lodge shone small and bright in the distance. I wanted to go back and have another drink. I turned back to the desert to call to Amberly.

But she was gone.

"Amberly," I called.

"Amberly," I called louder.

The windless desert extended silently in all directions, the black earth overhung by a gray night sky.

I listened for some sound beyond the clacking of my shoes against rock. Nothing. I stopped walking. I heard nothing.

The yellow and blue lights of the motor lodge flickered over my shoulder. I did not want to go any further into the dark and lose that light.

"Amberly," I screamed.

The desert made no sound. It was as if the barren earth held its breath, waiting for me to give up. I scanned the horizon, but there was no sign of her. I felt cold and alone.

I turned around and walked back to the lodge.

As I got close to Bungalow C, I tripped and fell to the ground. I landed on my knee and the pain spiked through the drunkenness and I yelped. I turned around to see if maybe Amberly had heard, to see if maybe she would come back. But there was nothing behind me but rock and sky.

I limped up to the bungalow and threw open the door. Easing inside, I called, "Amberly?"

The bungalow answered back with empty silence. Still, I limped through each room just to be sure. Nothing.

Back in the den, I peeked out the window at the office. The lights were still on, but no one seemed to be eavesdropping at the door. I didn't know if Delmer and the old woman had heard our fight, but if they had they didn't seem to care.

I plopped down in a chair and poured myself another drink. I felt like hell. I wanted to drown that hell in booze until the fire went out.

She'd come back. What choice did she have? There was nothing out there, for God's sake. Just nothing at all.

I drank the rotgut like it was some kind of penance. I lay my head back and tried not to think.

But I did think.

I thought of the women I'd known. There had been many. Some sad, some happy, some disturbed and lost and alone. I'd drifted through their lives and they had drifted through mine. Had I meant anything to them? Jesus, had they meant anything to me? Were we all just victims of each other? Or were none of us victims? I liked that idea better. It went down well. Yes, no one is really a victim.

I had another drink to celebrate, and I rubbed my throbbing knee.

"Amberly," I said to the empty room.

Hollywood. I had to go back there and turn in the car and the film stock. And then I was on the streets. Me and Amberly were on the streets, if she came back. Would she? She had to. Where could she go? There was nothing out there but the Goddamn desert. She would come back and I would say I was sorry and that she was more beautiful than Ingrid Bergman and funnier than Carole Lombard and she could sing better than Judy Garland. If she would just come back I would tell her all of that.

I stumbled to the door and opened it and looked out at the courtyard. I closed the door and had another drink.

I had tried fooling around with a man once. It was

like kissing a horse. I thought he was going to eat my face. And as for the sex – it was like trying to get that same horse to tap dance.

The first time I ever kissed a woman my whole body shook with fear, fear of a good kind. The kind of fear that comes from daring to hope in spite of all the reasons not to hope.

"Amberly ..." I moaned.

She had to come back. She had nowhere to go. She had nowhere to go.

I sat up. Delmer or the old lady, one of them had said there was a town. Of course, Brittle Rock. Yes, she went to Brittle Rock.

One more drink and I was in the car. I lit a cigarette to keep me awake.

The headlights barreled through the night, dust swarming around the car like bees, a high pitched whistle coming through some dent in the car.

White figure. Amberly. Road. Swerve.

Thump.

Brakes.

I stumbled out and the dust swept over me.

No.

But she wasn't there. I searched. Blinking in the cold, the car motor running.

I yelled her name into the darkness. I limped back down the road, calling her name.

Nothing.

She had to come back.

I called her name.

Nothing.

~ ~ ~

I woke up the next morning and leaned out of the car and vomited into the dirt. Then I stumbled out of the car and tried to stand up straight. The sun had already risen, flooding the sky with light and flooding my eyeballs until they threatened to burst.

I held onto the sides of my head like the whole thing might come apart.

I was in the desert, off the road somewhere. Ugly brush and cacti poked through the craggy dirt and rocks. I shut my eyes and tried to think.

Amberly.

I opened my eyes and ran to the front of the car.

Nothing. No blood. No new dent or shattered glass. Just dirt and grime from the road.

I almost cried at that. I got back into the car and started the engine and pulled away from my resting spot toward what I thought might be the general direction of the road.

I found it within a few minutes, and I went south, back toward the motor lodge. I'd driven for perhaps half a mile when I saw her on the side of the road.

She was laying in the ditch, down a gentle slope from the road. If you weren't looking in that exact spot at that exact moment it would be easy to miss her. I suppose some part of me *was* looking, some part of me knew where I would find her.

She lay flat on her back, still unblemished from the sun or insects, the ends of the scarf floating up like wisps of white smoke. A thin layer of dirt dusted her hair and skin, but aside from a single wad of red blood in her left nostril, she looked peaceful and composed, as if she'd stopped for a rest. I almost said her name, but I didn't.

Her eyes were closed, as if she'd been struck by the car and then crawled into the ditch to lay down and die.

I sat on a rock. I did not cry. I thought I would. I thought I should. But there were no tears in me.

I stood up and looked both ways down the road. It was early yet, but soon people would pass by and they would see her.

Unless I moved her.

Chapter Eighteen

I was miles away before I began to think. There was so much I did not want to think about. About the grave I had dug under the rising sun. About digging in the hard red earth with the lid of a film canister, digging and digging until my fingers bled and the canister was bent to hell. About the way the desert seemed to reject the offering I made it, refusing to let me penetrate the land more than a few inches down. About the shallow grave, miles away from the road, where I laid Amberly down and wrapped her head in the scarf and covered her in dirt and rocks. I did not want to think about her lying there, alone and unknown.

I did not want to think about going back to the Days And Nights Motor Lodge, about showering in the room, about watching the dirt from Amberly's grave run down the drain with the blood from my hands. I did not want to think about the story I told Delmer and the old woman about Amberly at the café having breakfast. I did not want to think about the fake laughter I had to muster at some stupid joke from Delmer as I said goodbye.

I did not want to think about any of it.

Instead, I drove. I drove just to get away from what I'd done, to put miles between me and the dead woman lying in her lonely desert grave.

But I saw death everywhere now. Eventually I had to stop to eat, and at a restaurant in Arizona I looked down at my plate and realized that everything on it was dead. Plants and animals had been plucked and slaughtered and I was feasting on the corpses of once living things.

The men and women I saw at the other tables, the children I saw playing in front of the courthouse as I walked back to my car, all of them would die, would rot in the earth like Amberly and would one day be as unknown as if they'd never lived at all.

The history of the world was the history of death. It was the end result of every life. It was the end result of life itself. We'd just come through a war that had killed millions of people and for what? So that we could wake up one morning to find that we might all die in an atomic fire from the sky. And if the fire didn't fall, if we managed to avoid that fate indefinitely, what of it? Annihilation only lay a little further down the road. We're all born to die.

~ ~ ~

Exhausted, I stopped somewhere in California and bought a bottle and drank myself into unconsciousness in a cheap hotel room. I awoke hours later in the dark and stumbled to the washroom down the hall and drank water out of the faucet. I threw up. I drank more water. Then I fell asleep on the floor.

Daylight came and I bought another bottle. I drank it. I passed out. I woke up and drank water. I ate some food. I bought another bottle and some cigarettes. I drank and smoked. I passed out.

I woke up in the dark. A man and a woman fought outside under a lamp. The woman said the man was a bum. The man said the woman was a whore. Someone up the street yelled down that they were both right. People laughed. The woman began to cry. I drank what was left of the bottle and passed out.

Daylight again. I threw up. I drank water. I hobbled to the liquor store. Closed. I waited until it opened. Children stared at me while their mothers averted their eyes. The store opened. The man there called me sweetheart and tried to talk me out of buying another bottle. I railed against fascism and the destruction wrought by cruel men. I claimed to have been a nurse in the war, to have held dying men as they cried for their mothers. I demanded a bottle for the memory of those young men. The man sold me the bottle and told me to never come back.

I climbed the stairs to my room. I drank. I passed out.

Sometime in the early evening, a skinny young man came to the door. He had a plump red pimple on the tip of his nose, like a tiny clown nose. He told me I had to pay more money or leave. I told him I did not have any more money. He told me I had to leave. I told him he could have sex with me if he let me stay. He got mad and said he was a Christian Scientist and that I would have to leave immediately.

My brain seemed to be trying to force its way out of my head as I gathered my things and stumbled out to the car.

I drove to the next town and pulled up to a roller skating rink. The place was packed with families and couples and youngsters. I walked around. Leaning against the rink in her skates, a chubby young woman wore jeans and a red checkered work shirt. I walked up to her and said hello.

She looked me up and down without saying hello. Finally, she asked me if I had a cigarette. I gave her one.

I asked her name. She told me her name was Samantha but that her friends called her Sammy. I asked if we were friends.

As I did, an older man came up. Tall and thin, with dark, sunken eyes, he looked like a mortician. He asked me why I was talking to his daughter. I said I was just saying hello. He told me to scram. I told him to fuck off. He turned red and started shouting.

People were looking at me now. I told them all to fuck off. The police came. I slugged one. They dropped me on the ground and put cuffs on me.

They threw me in the women's drunk tank with three other misunderstood ladies. One was black, and the other two were Mexicans. The Mexican girls weren't together. No one said anything. We all sat in different corners. We were in there for a couple of hours, but then a big ruckus started. There had been some kind of free-for-all at one of the honky-tonks in town, and the police needed overflow for the men. Me and the other broads were all booted out and told to go home and dry out.

I walked two miles back to my car, got in, and drove home to Los Angeles.

~ ~ ~

I parked in the garage, and the night man – a friendly fellow named Leroy – was polishing one of the cars. Leroy would polish up a car for two bits, and just about everyone who lived in the Chateau Michel paid him to do so. As a result, the man was always polishing a car. I don't think I'd ever seen him without a rag in his hand.

As I pulled into my spot, he walked over.

I'd just opened my door when he said, "Howdy, Miss Dixon. Back from your trip?"

"What?"

"Your trip to ..." he stopped to look me over. He was a middle-aged man with an alcoholic pallor to his skin that I'd never noticed before. "You been drinking, miss?"

I didn't know what to say to that. It was so forward, it stunned me a little.

He smiled. "Sorry if that seems like an abrupt question. You just don't look so swell. And you ... well, I hope you don't mind me saying, but you smell pretty strong of whiskey."

"You thirsty, Leroy? You want some?"

It was the first time I'd ever snapped at him, and he shrunk back a little, aware now that he'd overstepped. He put up his hands. "I'm just concerned is all. Didn't mean anything by it. Just came over to see if you wanted me to wash your car."

I stared at my car. The rolling instrument of death was filthy, caked in dirt and mud.

"No," I said. "You just leave it alone. I like it this way."

"Okay," he said. "I hope you have a pleasant evening."

I nodded and he backed away, returning to whatever sweet simplicity is found in wiping down hubcaps.

I left my luggage in the car and rode up the escalator. It hummed quietly. When it released me onto my floor, I was happy to find that my neighbors didn't appear to be home. I walked to my door and dug out my key. I unlocked it and stepped inside.

The first thing I noticed was that there was no mail piled up. The second thing I noticed was that Lucy and Eustace Harington were standing in my den.

Part Three:
The Woman From Arkansas
Winter, 1947

Chapter Nineteen

Lucy wore jeans, boots, and a blue checkered shirt. Her hair was pinned back. Her hands were at her sides.

"Eustace, go stand by the door," she said.

Eustace moved much more quickly than I would have thought. In a couple of steps, he was beside me, his hand easing the door shut. He didn't crowd me, but he smelled of old sweat.

I just stood there looking up at him. Finally I said, "Howdy, Eustace."

He grinned and nodded at me and then looked to his sister for guidance.

"Want to sit down, Billie?" Lucy asked. "You've had a long ride."

"So have you," I said.

She grinned. "We've been here a little while. You took the long way home."

"Yeah," I said. I walked into my apartment. It felt very distant from me. The furniture, the pictures on the wall – none of it seemed like it belonged to me. It was odd, but at that moment somehow the only part of the apartment that felt familiar were the Haringtons.

I walked past her to the window. "Actually, I don't feel like sitting down," I said. "I've been sitting for hours."

I looked down on some trees below my window.

Lucy waited. For a while, the only sound in the apartment was Eustace breathing through his mouth.

I said, "I don't suppose you're on vacation."

"No."

"Just came to visit Hollywood and decided to drop

153

in and see me?"

"No."

"Why are you here then?"

"We're here to take you back to Stock's Settlement to stand trial for the murder of Obadiah Henshaw."

I nodded. "Yeah. That will be a bit of a problem since you can't arrest me in California."

"I didn't say we were going to arrest you, Billie. I said we were going to bring you back."

I turned around and felt the cool glass of the window against my back. "That's kidnapping, Lucy. From this spot where we're standing all the way to the Arkansas state line, you're just kidnapping me."

She shook her head, smiling. "You're giving us too much jurisdiction, Billie. Eustace is just the sheriff of Connor County. We won't be on legal ground until we hit the county line."

"But you still think you can do it?"

"We didn't drive all the way to Los Angeles to see the palm trees. Which are very lovely, by the way. We've had quite a remarkable journey."

I walked over to the couch and sat down. My head throbbed and my body was depleted. All I really wanted to do was go back to sleep.

"You look bad," Lucy said.

"You know, you're the second person to tell me that in the last few minutes."

"Who was the other?"

"The night man in the garage."

"Not Amberly?"

I let that sink in. I looked up at her. "I haven't seen Amberly since I left Arkansas."

"Is that a fact?"

She walked over and sat down on the divan across from me. She looked natural in the jeans, but she still crossed her legs in a ladylike fashion.

"You're not as inconspicuous as you think, Billie. Two women travelling alone on Route 66. Driving a big car. Amberly is very pretty. People notice her. You're also pretty in your way, and you wear pants. It draws attention. People make note. People remember. A waitress. A motor lodge owner."

I stared at her. My head hurt worse. I rubbed my temples. Eustace hadn't moved from beside the door, and I could hear him breathing behind me.

"I didn't murder Obadiah Henshaw," I said.

Lucy looked at the space between us as if she were watching my words float in the air like fairies. "I see," she said. "Well, you sure did take a long time to say that. Instead, you went right to the 'you can't arrest me' defense."

"They already held an inquest and said I killed him on accident."

"They've changed their minds."

"How did that happen?"

"I changed their minds."

"Why?"

"Because I know you killed him."

"How?"

Lucy pondered the purpose of my question. I saw her debating whether or not she wanted to show me all her cards yet. I suppose she came to the conclusion that it couldn't do any harm, because she said, "After you left with Amberly, the whole town started talking. It was a mistake, Billie. Of all the things you could have done, you chose the very worst one. You ran off with the preacher's wife." She shook her head. "I must admit, I was stunned. When I heard – when old Mrs. Whittle from the church came to the office to tell me – I just sat there with my mouth open. The thing that stunned me the most is that you would be so brazen about it. That's almost the greater sin in the eyes of the good people of our town. To kill a man and steal his wife, that's a sin as old as David and Bathsheba. Granted, you put your own feminine spin on the story, but it was doing it so audaciously ... that's the thing people won't forgive."

I leaned back into the cushions of my couch, shut my eyes and rubbed my temples. "I'm sorry you're offended, Lucy."

"The thing that offends me is that you murdered a man."

"I didn't murder anyone."

"I found the log."

I opened my eyes. "What?"

"That you threw down the crevice. I found it. That's what I did with the day before we left. I went back out to the scene and looked around. Found it down there in the crevice caught between a couple of rocks, shielded from the elements. Still had a fragment of his scalp and hair on it."

"I ..."

She held up a hand to stop me. "You have plenty of time to try and come up with a defense. You have the entire trip back to Arkansas to come up with something."

I sat up. She leaned forward. It was as if we had locked eyes over a chess board. I said, "What's to keep me from screaming for help right now?"

"Two things. One, if you try, Eustace is going to thump your head. He won't like doing it. He never likes hitting a lady. But he'll do it just the same. And that's going to give you an even worse headache than the one you clearly already have. And number two, it wouldn't do you any good. Might slow things down for a couple of days. Might. Might not. We have a warrant for your arrest. Sure, we don't have jurisdiction, but these Los Angeles police officers have their own crimes to solve. Unless you're wanted for something here, I doubt they would kick up much of a fuss about extraditing you back to Arkansas."

That took the wind out of me. I sat back, and my body seemed to deflate. Lucy watched me. She glanced up at her brother and nodded. He walked over and sat down next to her on the divan.

I tried to think of something to say, but my mind was blank. I could barely hold myself up, and I couldn't think very well. I don't know if it was fear, depression, or just plain exhaustion, but I could barely keep myself upright anymore. I said, "I'm tired ..."

Lucy nodded. "Get some sleep." She turned to her brother. "We'll leave in the morning."

~ ~ ~

With the sun breaking through my blinds, I woke up in my bed the next morning. The room was cool and quiet, with the light slowly starting to fill the room. I sat up in bed and found that Eustace was sitting in a chair across the room.

As I blinked at him, he just stared at me. Eustace had a way of going blank. He was like a sheet of paper with nothing written on it. I would have been more alarmed to find him in my room if he'd had any expression at all – one of menace, annoyance, or even happiness. All of that would have given me the creeps. But Eustace never seemed to be doing anything except waiting to be told what to do.

"Good morning," I said.

He smiled and nodded.

"Where's your sister?"

Blank stare.

"Where's Lucy?"

Nothing.

"Can I get up and use the powder room?"

Smile. Nod.

I slid out of bed. I was wearing my pajamas. I vaguely remembered putting them on the night before, but I'd fallen asleep almost immediately.

I walked across the room to my bath and closed the door. In the mirror over my sink, my face seemed strange, like the face of an unknown actor on a movie screen. It's an odd thing to watch yourself as you watch yourself – it was like two images staring at each other. All that seeing, but who was really doing the looking? I looked down at my hands, the nicked knuckles and nubby fingernails. They seemed like foreign objects. Had these hands really buried Amberly?

I used the toilet and brushed my teeth and splashed my face with water. When I walked back out into the bedroom, Eustace was gone and the door was open. I walked over to the door and peaked through.

Across the den, from the kitchen Lucy looked up and saw me and said, "Good morning."

I walked out into the den. The place smelled of bacon and eggs.

"Did you go shopping this morning?"

"I did. I also made breakfast. Get dressed. We'll eat and get on the road."

I scratched my head. "Okay."

~ ~ ~

They were driving a Coupe that was a few years old.

"It's the doctor's car," Lucy explained. "He felt bad about botching the inquest. Loaned it to the city. City's paying the expenses. I have to keep our travel accounts in good order."

Eustace had taken a shower in my bathroom. When he came out, he was fully dressed, but his face was pink and his hair still dripping. As he loaded my suitcase into the Ford, Lucy smiled and joshed him,

"You smell like a girl."

He grinned and held up his hand and she smelled his tanned skin. They smiled at each other.

It was such a sweet moment between them that I decided to make a run for it. I slipped away while they were still smiling at each other.

I was wearing slacks and a man's checked shirt and some good shoes. Without looking behind me, I ran down the street, passing parked cars and people waiting for the bus. The sidewalks seemed too open, so I ducked down a long sunny alley with a fence at the end. I hopped on top of a garbage bin and pulled myself over the fence. Then I ducked into a restaurant on the corner that was still serving breakfast. The place was bustling and no one noticed me as I headed for the ladies' room.

Inside, I sat down in a stall and waited. A woman came in, used the other stall, and washed up. A woman came in with two little boys and washed syrup off their hands and butter off their mouths. A girl came in and blew her nose and left without washing her hands.

Eventually, I eased out. The bathroom was empty. I eased further out into the restaurant. It had switched to lunch.

I made my way to the door.

"Hey."

I turned around.

The lady behind the counter said, "You going to get something to eat or what?"

I shook my head and left. Outside, the day was clear and bright. I took two steps and ran into Eustace. He took my arm and led me to the side of the building where Lucy was waiting in the Ford.

He put me in the backseat. Lucy turned around. She didn't seem mad or upset with me. It was as if we'd eaten at the restaurant and she'd had been waiting for me to finish paying the check.

"Hands," she said.

I held up my hands. She put cuffs on me.

Eustace slid into the back with me.

"Now that we got that out of the way," Lucy said, turning around and settling into the seat. "Let's go home."

Chapter Twenty

Our first day on the road, Eustace sat beside me in the backseat. That day I realized I had been wrong when I assumed he never knew what was going on. He never spoke and rarely made any sound, but he was always paying attention. Near the end of the day, I was staring at the road running by when he leaned over and tapped my shoulder. He gestured at the sky, crystal blue and fractured by streaks of red from the sinking sun. Together we just stared at the warm glow spreading out across the horizon. After the sun dipped below the earth, Eustace turned to me and smiled in the dying light.

Lucy held her own surprises. The next day she let me sit up front, and as we rolled through the southwest we talked. At first, it was small talk about birds we saw, or cars we passed, or people walking on the side of the road.

But soon enough I learned that Lucy wasn't much for small talk. That's not to say that she wasn't a talker. Quite the opposite was true. She just had very little patience for talk that was essentially meaningless. She was a talker who was interested in meaningful things.

"I've never been too sure about the existence of God," she told me. We were driving through the desert, Eustace sleeping in the back while we talked about one thing or another, and the subject had come up, naturally, in the easy way that serious subjects surface when you're talking to a serious person. "I grew up in Stock's Settlement, so of course I was taught to believe. I don't think my mother ever questioned God. She loved the King James Bible, though, and it's fair to say that she raised us on it. But she was never a dogmatic person. None of our people were ever fire-and-brimstoners as far as I can recall. They were believers, to every last man and woman, but I don't know that any of them ever believed it past the point of public decency."

"What do you mean by public decency?"

"No one in our family ever felt that religion was much more than a polite social obligation. Mother respected preachers, but she never seemed to lose sight of their humanity. She'd read the same book they had, and I don't think she ever believed that she'd met a man who had read it deeper or better or truer than she had. At the end of the day, a preacher is a man interpreting a text for you. Mother just went straight to the source."

"Quite a woman, your mother."

"She was," Lucy said with a smile. "But I hate to hog all the talk here. What about your people?"

I stared out at the passing desert, the cacti spearing up between hard rock and yellow-white dirt. "Not much to say. Daddy was a roughneck and a cowboy. He rode horses in the rodeo and drank tequila and chased women. He was with my mother just long enough to make me."

"Did she raise you?"

"No, she dropped me off at his mother's house on her way out of town. The way she saw it, it was the old lady's fault for raising such a worthless son. She certainly had no intention of sticking around being an unwed mother. She moved east to the Carolinas. Eventually, she got married and had a couple of children. And that was it for her. She's probably got a couple of grandkids of her own by now."

"You see much of your father?"

"He came back to town occasionally to see me and

grandma. He was all talk. Every time he came through, there was some new story. He'd stop by on his way to Colorado to work for a logging company. He'd kiss me on the forehead and tell me he was going to send for me. Then a couple of years would pass, and when he finally did show back up, he would have been in Utah working for Mormons or something. Always some new story. He was going to move to Hollywood to be a stuntman. Or he was going to be a crewman on a rich man's yacht. Always a new story, always about how the promised land was just over the horizon. For all I know, he actually believed it."

We rode in silence as Lucy pondered all I had told her. Finally she said, "I'm sorry to hear that, Billie."

I shrugged. I'd told that story before. Girls liked tragic tales of ne'er-do-well fathers. It didn't hurt that the tale was true – the old man hadn't been worth a damn – but I knew that the point of the story was that I'd had it rough.

Still, after she told me she was sorry for me, Lucy didn't say any more about it.

I could tell that she wasn't someone who was going to be swayed by my tale of woe.

"I imagine you've heard some sad stories in your time," I said.

She grinned and nodded. "In my line work...that is to say, in Eustace's line of work, you hear all manner of sad stories. This world has never wanted for sadness."

"So," I said, "I'm not going to get anywhere with you by crying."

She smiled at that. "If I've learned one thing, Billie," she said, "it's that tears should never convince anyone of anything."

~ ~ ~

She drove all day. As the sun started to darken the

west, she began looking for a place to stop for the night. I felt my heart sink when we topped a hill and plunged into a desert valley and I could see, in the distance, the gleaming blue and yellow lights of the Days And Nights Motor Lodge.

"I'd rather not stop there," I said.

Lucy said, "We're not going to stop there. There's a cheaper place in town."

We crossed the valley, the neon sign growing ever larger, and she turned off the road by the motor lodge and started toward Brittle Rock. I realized then that we were driving by Amberly's grave.

Is she doing this on purpose? I wondered. *She wants to see how I'll respond?*

The desert at night was as cool and dark and blue as it had been just a few days before. We passed cactuses and mounds of rocks, but I didn't remember where Amberly was buried out there.

We came to Brittle Rock. The city's streets were lined with one-story buildings on either side. A gas station at the corner. A leather shop. A knife shop. A diner. A surprising number of people milled about, and most of them seemed to be headed to the edge of town.

We pulled up to a small two-story hotel, and as we got out of the car and stretched our legs, I saw tents set up beside a small city park just down the street.

Lucy leaned forward and said, "What on earth?"

At first glance, I thought it was just a circus, but a large tasseled banner over the entrance to the circle of tents announced:

W.J. Wallace's Festival
of Unusual Attractions

From where we were, we couldn't see into any of the tents but we could see a large open-air elephant pen. A man with a long iron-gray beard and red velvet pants was giving rides on a haggard looking beast with sad eyes and dry, cracking skin. A line of families stood around the elephant pen waiting their turns.

A father paid the bearded man, and the man walked the elephant over to a rickety little ladder. The elephant took a knee, its massive, hairy trunk lying in the dirt like a depleted water hose, and three boys climbed up on its back.

I shook my head. The father laughed. The mother of the boys, watching her children slide around on top of the tired old beast, stood with one fist pressed to her chest and the other pressed to her mouth.

Lucy watched her brother. Eustace stood with his hands down and his mouth slung open.

A hot breeze flung some dirt against us, but we all just watched the man leading the elephant around the pen by a long leash.

The more I watched the hulking animal clomping around the pen, though, the odder I felt about it. Something about seeing that giant creature led around in circles as an attraction angered me.

I felt my face flush.

"Can we go inside already?" I asked.

Lucy turned to me. I don't know what she read on my face, but she nodded and said, "Eustace, let's go."

The big man stared at the elephant until his sister pulled at his sleeve.

We walked up the steps of the hotel.

"Have you ever seen an elephant before?" Lucy asked me.

"Sure. In Hollywood."

"We haven't. Not in the flesh, anyway. Seen them in photographs or jungle movies. Never up close like that."

"Yeah," I said, "it must be a big day for you."

She glanced at me, but she didn't respond.

Inside, a bucktoothed man with thick spectacles checked us in. "All we got left is a two room suite," he told us.

"That will be fine," Lucy said.

"Last thing available in the hotel, what with the geek show in town," he said. He stopped when he saw that I was wearing handcuffs.

I waved at him. "You got your own little geek show right here."

Lucy handed the man a piece of paper and explained that she and Eustace were extraditing me back to Arkansas to stand trial for a felony offense. The hotel clerk thought that was wonderful, and his bulging, magnified eyes looked me up and down like I was an escaped oddity from W.J. Wallace's Festival.

He led us down the hall to a suite. It was a spacious two bed set up. He said, "The washroom is back down the hall." Then his big weird eyes gave me one more hungry gawking, and he left.

Lucy told Eustace, "I need to visit the washroom."

He nodded.

She left without saying anything to me. I hadn't meant to insult her outside, but I knew it had been taken that way. I thought about apologizing, but as soon as I had the thought I rejected it. This woman was taking me to jail. Why the hell should I care about her feelings or her pride? What she was doing was illegal, transporting me this way, across state lines. It was kidnapping. And for what? She couldn't prove that I had murdered the preacher. She didn't even know that Amberly was dead.

The more I sat and thought about it, the madder I got. My life had been one long unbroken string of misfortunes. Bad luck and betrayal had snapped at my feet my whole life. I cursed the day I ever entered the state of Arkansas. I cursed the day I ever took a job at PRC. I would have been better off getting another waitressing job.

I told the big man, "Eustace, I need to change for bed."

He just stared at me as I lifted my suitcase and took it into the other room. I put the suitcase on the bed and closed the door behind me.

Then I walked over to the window and opened it and climbed out into the night.

Chapter Twenty-One

I ran behind the hotel toward the geek show. I had no plan. I had no thought except to get away. Sweat covered my face and my heart kicked against my chest.

Hide in the tents. Hide until you can find a way to cut the handcuffs.

Maybe Lucy would think that I had run toward the desert. *Hide in the tents.*

The place got louder as I got closer. Kids yelling about that sad elephant. Teenagers yelling about the geeks in the back tents. Barkers trying to sell trinkets and popcorn. I passed by a trash bin. Inside was half-eaten food and used napkins and balled up paper sacks. Nothing I could use to obscure the handcuffs.

I got to the entrance of W.J. Wallace's Festival of Unusual Attractions and walked past the people in line to the fat old man taking tickets at the gate. I held up my handcuffs. "I'm the new escape artist," I said.

He had a round red face and dumb brown eyes. "Pardon?"

"I'm the new escape artist," I said, bouncing on my feet and waving my handcuffs at him. "I got to get in there. I stepped out to use the shithouse, and now I need to get back in."

He said, "Well, go on in."

I went in, looking over my shoulder back at the hotel up the street. So far, nothing.

Lanterns hung on wires between the tents, and people lined up under the swaying lights, waiting to get into the attractions marked **Restricted To Adults**. The largest tent promised **All Manner Of Body Oddities**. Another advertised **Catherine The**

Uncanny Contortionist. The smallest tent, which had the longest line, simply said **The Rat Eater**.

I hurried past the tents to the caravan of large trucks sitting in the darkness. I crawled under one and sat there in the cold dirt, waiting in the shadows for the freak show to end. Once they packed up, I would crawl inside one of the trucks and hide.

From where I lay balled up behind the large wheel of the truck, I couldn't see very much. I couldn't see the entrance to the grounds, and I couldn't really make out the faces of any of the people walking into or leaving the tents.

If I had possessed the presence of mind to cry, I suppose I would have. My life was over. No matter what happened next, my life as I'd always known it would be altered beyond all comprehension.

But I didn't cry. I waited. I watched for Lucy or Eustace or a local sheriff. All I saw were the people of Brittle Rock, though. The kids and their parents were all near the front, by the elephant and a juggling clown. The teenagers and the rowdies all drifted back toward the adult tents.

A scream went up inside the tent of the Rat Eater. After a moment, the flap burst open and a young woman ran out, followed soon after by a young man who rushed to catch up to her. The people waiting in line laughed nervously, but none of them got out of line.

Behind me, a wind blew across the desert and pelted my face with dirt. I squeezed my eyes shut and covered my mouth and nose. The winds kept blowing, so I curled up with my hands covering my face.

I thought of Amberly. I couldn't help but think of her, buried just a few miles away, not far off the road, exposed to the onslaught of vermin and ants. It was as if she was sending these bitter winds against me to drive me from my hiding place.

The winds blew harder. I balled up as tightly as I could.

In a few moments – if it had not happened already – everyone in Brittle Rock would know I was missing. Then I would be found. There was nowhere for me to hide in this tiny town. I would be found, or I could flee into the desert.

As if in answer to that thought, the coarse wind tore at my hands and ears and neck and arms.

What are you running from? Your punishment? But why? Don't you deserve it? Amberly was out there right now, her flesh already coming apart under the cruel teeth of nature. Wasn't the same thing going to happen to me, no matter what? I could never run so far or so fast that I could outrun what was coming for me eventually.

The wind screamed across the empty wasteland hurling dirt and rocks at me. I could not lay there anymore and take the beating from the desert. I would have to climb into the truck.

I pushed myself out into the lantern light for just a moment, but as soon as I climbed to my feet Lucy was there.

"Eustace," she said.

Eustace slugged me in the back of the head and everything went bright red and then navy blue and then black.

I was awake before I hit the ground, but now I was wobbly and had the beginnings of a pounding headache. Eustace held me up like I was drunk, and Lucy led us back to the hotel.

~ ~ ~

Lucy chained me to the radiator that night. She had Eustace push the bed over, had me stick out my foot, and she clapped a leg iron on my ankle. I could lay down, and I slept fine.

~ ~ ~

The next morning we were on the road again, all three of us in the front seat. Neither of them had really spoken to me since the bad business the day before. Lucy had issued orders and Eustace and I had followed her instructions without comment. Of course, Eustace never commented on anything, but now I followed his lead. If anyone had observed us, they would have thought that Eustace and I were Lucy's mute servants.

After half a day of that, however, the silence got to be too much for me. I can't go that long without talking.

"Sorry about yesterday," I said.

Lucy grinned. "Oh yes?"

"Yes."

"Well, I appreciate you saying it. I'd appreciate it more, though, if you don't try that again."

I nodded. "What about Eustace? Think he forgives me?"

Lucy looked across me at Eustace. "Do you forgive her?"

He stuck out his bottom lip.

"Hmm. I don't think he forgives you, Billie."

I looked up at him. I felt like the mouse sitting next to the lion. "Hell, Eustace, I said I was sorry."

Lucy said, "I think he's mad you tried to escape. I told you, he doesn't like to hit women."

"Aw, c'mon, Eustace," I said. "Can you blame me? I'm on my way to the big house, for Christ's sake."

He didn't look at me. His big wet lip just hung there.

"I panicked," I said. "That's all. Nothing personal. Hell, I don't hold it against you for slugging me in the head."

He turned and looked out the passenger side window.

I turned to Lucy.

She lifted her fingers off the wheel as if it say, *It's out of my hands.*

I said, "You country folk sure do hold a grudge."

She smiled. "Just give him a little time to sit with it."

"Okay," I said. I poked his arm. "But I'm not giving up on you, Eustace."

We rode for a while. We passed into Oklahoma. I felt my breath get a little tighter. It wouldn't be too many hours now and we would be back in Stock's Settlement. I tried not to think about that.

Lucy was watching me from the corner of her eye, but she didn't say anything.

I said, "Have you caught many – have you arrested many people for murder?"

"No," she said. "Pretty quiet town. We mostly settle down drunks and resolve petty disputes before they turn into something big."

"Do you like the job?"

Lucy thought about that for a moment. "In our town, it's the best one available to me."

"Ever think about moving away?"

Lucy held the wheel with both hands. She said, "I don't know where we would go. If we were going to move away, we should have done it a long time ago after our parents passed away."

We stopped talking and the only sound in the car was the hum of the wheels on the pavement.

Finally Lucy said, "In some respects ... I think I admire you, Billie."

"Why?"

"You tried. At least you tried."

"I failed."

"That's true," she said. "Still, it's better to have loved and lost than never to have loved at all."

"Is that a quote from something?"

"Tennyson."

"I never saw it."

She smiled. Then she laughed. "You're a character, Billie." She kept chuckling. "You're a real character."

"Be sure to mention that to the court."

Her mouth tightened. She stared straight ahead, her strong hands clutching the wheel. After that, she didn't seem to want to talk anymore.

~ ~ ~

Winter had arrived early. Frost covered eastern Oklahoma and western Missouri, and by the time we turned off Route 66 and crossed into Arkansas the world had turned crystal. As we wound our way down into the Ozarks, the crooked mountain paths that had so vexed me on my first trip through the region now seemed tame in comparison to the icy sliver of road we had to drive. No rail protected us from slipping off the road, no embankment existed to keep us from plunging through those shimmering treetops far below us to the frozen creek bed glistening at the bottom of the gorge.

Lucy said nothing as she navigated this dicey corridor between cold rock and bottomless eternity. She handled the Ford as well as anyone could, but I didn't know what we would do if a car suddenly appeared coming up that narrow path. Like Lucy, I kept my eyes forward, locked on those few feet of road we could see before it disappeared around the bend.

~ ~ ~

The setting sun was at our backs as we finally rounded the curve and saw Stock's Settlement below us. Beside me, Eustace smiled at the sight of his hometown. I could feel him relax for the first time since they'd abducted me in California.

Lucy, however, did not seem relaxed – though she certainly had every reason to want to rest. She had been on the road for days and had driven every mile of the way, including the brutal last leg of the journey, yet I hadn't seen her flag or get drowsy. I hadn't felt her lose focus. The further we drove into town, however, the more she seemed to tense up.

She took a deep breath.

"Are you okay?" I asked.

She raised her eyebrows. "I suppose I should ask you that. You're the one in trouble, now."

It was true, of course. I was the one staring down the possibility of spending the rest of my life in jail, but at that moment I wasn't scared. Since Eustace had bopped me on the head, I hadn't thought about escaping. I hadn't dwelled on the future at all, in fact.

We rounded Appleton Avenue and people on the side of the road turned and watched us. We got downtown and Lucy pulled up next to the jail. She got out and stretched. Eustace got out the other side, reached back in and gently pulled me into the biting winter wind.

I'd barely taken my first step through the snow when I realized that it had already begun. People appeared at the doors of businesses, faces pressed against windows. At Dub's, I saw Helen holding a broom. From across the street I could see what she said, the same thing that everyone was saying: "They got her. They got Billie Dixon."

Chapter Twenty-Two

Two men were waiting on us inside the sheriff's office. For Stock's Settlement, they were both fairly well dressed. The one leaning against the wall was Brother Nathan Pickett, the preacher who'd baptized me. He knew me, of course, but he didn't regard me at all. Instead, he looked at the other man who was sitting at Lucy's desk – a dark-haired, lean man with unblinking close-set eyes. With one look, I knew that they must be brothers.

The man at the desk said, "Well lookee what the sheriff dragged in."

Lucy stepped in front of me. "Howdy, Lionel. Making yourself at home in our office?"

Lionel Pickett said, "Well now, Lucy, no one seems to be using it. You and the, uh, sheriff being out of town so long, me and Nathan just figured that we should come by and keep the place nailed down."

Behind him, Brother Pickett said, "We figured it could use a man's touch." He looked at Lionel to see if Lionel thought his joke was funny. Lionel laughed, and Nathan beamed.

Lucy nodded and looked down at her hands. "Well, we sure do appreciate it." She nodded at the large cast-iron stove in the corner of the room and said, "And you warmed the place up for us. I appreciate that as well."

Eustace held me by the arm and looked at his sister. I couldn't tell if he was worried, but he held my arm tight – not like he was afraid I would run but like he was afraid these men might try to steal me.

Lionel ignored the comment about the stove. "Looks awful bad, Lucy," he said. "Awful bad.

Preacher gets runned over and the killer escapes into the night with the man's wife. And you and your brother let it all happen under your noses. Don't hardly look right."

We had actually escaped first thing in the morning, but I kept that to myself.

Lucy said, "Y'all drop by to point that out to me?"

Lionel stood up and walked around the desk. "Naw. Like I said, we just come by because the place looked untended."

"I made it very well known we were going after her," Lucy said.

He nodded vigorously. "Oh that's true. That's true. You surely did. And here you are, with the fugitive by the arm. Well done. I salute you for it, and I hope the good people of this town will appreciate the fine work you done. Course now, they'll have to forgive you for letting it all happen in the first place, but I reckon you can talk your way out of that."

"Well," Lucy said, "thanks so much for showing your concern."

Lionel nodded and placed a hand to his breast. "We are just trying to give you the support you need."

Brother Pickett said, "We're just trying to be proper Christians."

"That's right, that's right," Lionel said, as if his brother had just reminded him of a chore that needed tending to. "We're just trying to be proper Christians."

Without responding to that, Lucy turned to her brother and said, "Eustace, why don't you take her back to the cell. We'll let these boys go on home."

"We wouldn't mind staying," Lionel said, raising a hand to stop Eustace. "Y'all must be in desperate need of some shut eye."

Eustace looked to his sister.

She told the men. "We're fine. You can both go on

178

home. Rest assured, we will send word if we need you."

She said it with a smile, but she said it pointedly enough that both of the men nodded. "Alrighty then," Lionel said. "I expect we'll see y'all later."

"I'm sure of it," Lucy said.

They walked to the door. Brother Pickett went out first, but Lionel paused there a moment, looked back and said, "You *can* be sure of it."

Then he left.

In the course of their conversation, none of them had spoken a word to me.

~ ~ ~

Eustace took me through a doorway at the back of the office and into a cold room with a gray metal cage in the center. Inside the cage was an old army cot with a folded blanket and a pillow.

Lucy drew out a key and unlocked the cage and I stepped inside. She locked the cage behind me.

I leaned on the bars.

"How many Pickett brothers are there?" I asked. "I remember the prosecuting attorney, and I recognize the preacher who dunked me in a horse trough. Lionel is a new one."

"There's three Pickett brothers," she said. "Though why I should come back to find those two here is something of a mystery. I sent a telegraph to let folks know we were coming back, but I didn't expect to find the Pickett boys waiting for us."

"Lionel seems like the brains in the family."

She leaned against the bars and rubbed her eyes. "He's the oldest brother. He doesn't exactly run the other two, but he's definitely the oldest brother, if you follow my meaning. Right now he owns and operates Pickett's Dry Goods. You been in there?"

"I can't say that I have."

She motioned in the general direction of Main Street. "Over by Tharp's Barbershop." She stopped and looked back over her shoulder. Then she said, almost to herself, "Lionel took over the store when he came home from the Pacific. I wonder if maybe he's getting bored with it."

"What do you mean?"

She rubbed her eyes again. "Doesn't matter."

Out in the office, the front door opened. Presently, three men entered the room. I recognized them all from the inquest. One was Josiah Pickett, the fat prosecuting attorney. The man behind him was the judge. The last man, stinking and silent, was my little defense attorney, Mr. Oglesby.

Josiah Pickett dabbed some sweat from his face even though the room was still cold and the weather outside was even worse. "Well, thank goodness you got her," he said.

Lucy nodded. "I said we would."

The judge lowered his chin and looked at me over his glasses. Staring at me like he was appraising a horse, he asked Lucy, "Where'd you get her?"

"Her apartment in California."

"Oo-ee," Josiah Pickett said. "That is an odyssey. All the way to California and back. Bet you want to hit the hay."

Lucy rubbed the back of her neck. "I'll allow I could use some rest."

Josiah Pickett dabbed his damp jowls and said, "I know Lionel and Nathan would be happy to come help out. They'd take the first watch while you and Eustace get some shut eye."

Lucy stood up straighter and pursed her lips. "Would they now? They told you that?"

"Well, yes, they volunteered to help."

"I expect they're still waiting out there," Lucy said,

"just in case they're needed."

"I'm proud to say that my brothers have been quite a help to this town while you been gone. Been watching this place."

"I see."

The judge looked over his glasses at her. "No need to take such an unladylike tone, Lucy. Weren't nobody minding the jail while you were gone, so Lionel kept watch. You might ought to have thought about that before you lit out after this gal. You ought to thank the Picketts instead of acting insulted."

The way he talked to her surprised me. I'd become accustomed to her as an authority figure, but in an instant her authority seemed to have been brushed aside. Even though Lucy was, for all intents and purposes, the sheriff of the town, the judge talked to her now like she was a wayward girl who'd stayed out too late.

Lucy blinked, but she held her tongue. She nodded. "Yes sir. I can see that that's right. Eustace and I were more focused on pursuit. I should have thought to ask someone to take over in our absence."

The judge nodded. "Well, if you feel like you got things in hand we'll leave."

"Yes sir. Eustace will take first watch, and I'll take over for him. If we need help, we'll let Josiah and his brothers know."

"Any time," Josiah Pickett said.

"Good girl," the judge said. "We'll take this up in the morning. This moves to the front of business for everybody. Tomorrow. Nine o'clock."

"Yes sir," Lucy said.

Once again, no one had spoken to me. Mr. Oglesby – who hadn't said a word – hadn't even looked in my direction.

Lucy walked them out to the front door and bid

them goodnight. After she closed and locked the door, she muttered something. It was too low for me to make it out, but it had the tone and tenor of a curse.

When she walked back in to my cell, she looked thoughtful.

"I'll leave this door open," she said. "We'll put some more wood on the fire. This room should heat up fairly well. You need anything, just holler."

"I will."

"Try and get some sleep."

"Lucy."

"Yes."

"What happens tomorrow?"

"We'll see," she said.

~ ~ ~

I passed a sleepless night in the cold, gray cell. The room never warmed up, but I considered that I had become too used to California winters. I'd gone soft.

I lay on the cot and wished that I could just fall asleep forever. To just fall away, to drift into nothingness ...

But I lay there awake and alert in the windowless dark, listening to Eustace snore at his desk while the wind shook the sides of the building. The only light came from the stove in the next room, one feeble yellow streak shivering on the floor and casting quivering shadows through the bars of my cage.

I thought of Amberly alone in the desert, asleep now in the earth. Had I ever really thought we could be together? Had I ever really thought there was a place in this world that would have allowed it? Had she? Perhaps she did, but more likely she just wanted to escape, to get away from this place. The town had seemed like it was prison. Her whole life had seemed like bondage, I suppose, and I must have seemed like a compatriot there to liberate her from her jailers. Did she love me, ever? Probably not. That thought had sent me into a rage just a few days before, but now it didn't. Now, as I looked at the gray walls and black bars of my cell, I knew that I would pledge love to anyone who might come to the door to rescue me. If that's how Amberly had regarded me, I couldn't really blame her.

Had I loved her? I think so. I had felt something like love, and that's really all we ever have to go on – that tangled mess of desire, fear, and need that we call love.

Now, though, love itself seemed so small. Had I really done such horrible things in pursuit of love? I wished I'd stayed in California. I wished I could wipe away the past. Obadiah and Amberly and all the rest of them.

Yet even as I lay there, I listened for Lucy to return. I didn't want to wipe her away. I knew she was the closest thing I had to a friend.

~ ~ ~

Somewhere in the night, she came back. The office door opened and her boots crept over the floorboards. I heard her gently wake her brother.

"You can go on home and get some sleep," she told him. "I'll be fine. You come back at seven-thirty. We'll get a bite to eat and then go over to the courthouse."

The big man moaned as he stretched and stood up. She walked him to the door and locked it behind him.

"Lucy," I said.

She appeared in the doorway. She wore a heavy coat, slacks and boots. "You're awake?"

"I can't sleep."

"That's understandable."

183

"Would you talk to me a bit?"

"Let me put on some more wood, and I'll come back."

She loaded up the stove and drug the desk chair back into the room and sat beside my cage.

"How are you faring in our little jail?"

"I find it unpleasant."

"That's the intended effect of the place, I reckon."

"Well, it's working."

She nodded and leaned back in her chair.

I said, "I'm surprised to see you in slacks."

"It's cold outside."

"I know, but I was told that ladies in Stock's Settlement did not wear britches."

"They do in the middle of the night in the howling wind." She tilted her head back at the office. "Besides, I have a change of clothes for the courthouse tomorrow."

"What will happen to me tomorrow, Lucy?"

She took a deep breath. "If I'm a fair judge of the general mood around here – and I think I am – I expect your case to move with lightening rapidity. The judge and prosecuting attorney have nothing better to do than try this case. They'll arraign you and call up a jury. If the judge is in a particularly dark mood, he'll start the trial. If he thinks his reputation is on the line, he'll finish the trial before supper."

"I don't even have a lawyer."

"Then he'll assign you Oglesby again."

"That little man who sat next to me at the inquest last time?"

"Yes. Bartholomew Oglesby. He's every bit as good a lawyer as you think he is."

"Oh my God."

The stove light flickering on her cheeks and chin gave her eyes a golden glint. "I'm afraid so, Billie. I don't take a lot of pleasure in telling you, but I thought you should know. Anything the judge regards as hindering the proceedings he'll wave away like he's shooing a fly off ice cream."

"Is there ... is there any chance I'll be found innocent? Are you saying the verdict is certain before a jury has even been called?"

She drew a deep breath. "It doesn't look good, Billie."

"But aside from a piece of wood you found nothing has changed," I said. "Nothing has changed since the last time I sat in that courtroom."

"Except you snuck out of town with the dead man's wife. We might be backwards, Billie, but we're not blind."

In the dark of my cell, where she could not see me, I closed my eyes. "Is that what people are saying?"

"People are talking. Angry whispers give rise to shouted indignation."

She turned and looked over her shoulder as though she'd heard a noise. When she turned back, however, her face revealed that she'd just realized something. "The Picketts," she said.

"What about them?"

"First Nathan baptized you. Then ole hopper-tailed Josiah ran the inquest that let you walk free. That's why all three of them showed up in my jail within a few minutes of us being back in town. They're afraid that they'll be blamed for letting you escape. Lionel knows he needs to put a good face forward to protect the family name, so he's been camped out here from the moment I pulled out of the city limits." She smiled grimly at that. "I bet he's been doing a lot of talking while Eustace and I have been gone. A lot of talking."

I suspected that she was thinking about her own

reputation, about the way the Picketts had been badmouthing her while she was chasing me down. At that moment, however, I cared more about how all of this affected my chances the next day.

"Tomorrow in court, what ... what will I get?"

"I expect you'll get a life sentence."

"Not death?"

She sat back in the chair. "Arkansas doesn't execute women. I don't think they've executed one in my lifetime."

"Other states do. California electrocuted a woman just this year."

"Yes, well, Arkansas takes a certain measure of pride in being different than California."

"So if not death ..."

She drew another long breath. "Like I said, it could be anything, Billie. You killed a man. A preacher. Ran him over like a dog and then ran off with his wife. That's an atrocity compounded by an affront. I don't think you should expect any kind of reprieve. I hate to put it so bluntly, but I'm just telling you what to expect."

I let that settle on me. Lucy watched the shadows on the wall.

"I wish I'd never met that woman," I said.

Lucy said nothing to that. She simply sat there with her hands on her lap.

I turned over on my cot and faced away from her. I stared into the darkest corner of the room. Its blackness comforted me. "Maybe death would be the only reprieve," I said.

Chapter Twenty-Three

Eustace showed up the next morning with biscuits and black coffee. I couldn't figure out how he'd come by them. Either he'd made them himself, or he'd stopped by Dub's before he came to the jail. But exactly how would he order biscuits and coffee? I didn't raise the question with Lucy, though, because she was too busy.

A little after daylight began filling the outer room, people had begun showing up at the jailhouse. I sat on the cot and listened as Lucy received a group of church ladies, followed by some men, followed by a delegation from the courthouse.

I didn't recognize any of the voices, and Lucy didn't bring anyone back to see me. One man asked if he could take a peek at me, but Lucy's voice dipped into a drawl when she told him, "This ain't a geek show, Tucker." Tucker made a crack about Lucy's lack of ladylikeness, but he left after that.

Eustace brought in my breakfast on a tin tray. He set the tray on the ground next to the cage, and I reached through the bars. I couldn't slide the tray through the bars without turning it vertical, so I just retrieved the biscuits and coffee and went back to my bunk to eat.

Lucy had changed into a gray-and-green striped chambray dress with a green belt and matching shoes. Somehow, she'd found the time to fix her hair. I wanted to tell her she looked nice, but it seemed like an odd thing to do under the circumstances.

"Would you like to wash up, Billie?" she asked.

"Yes, please," I said.

She opened the cage and showed me to the small

lavatory that seemed to be the only other room in the jailhouse. It was small and windowless, but it was comfortable enough. I used the toilet and splashed cold water over my face from the sink. Next to the sink was Lucy's hairbrush. I picked it up and used it to tame my hair.

Lucy knocked on the door.

I opened the door, the brush still in my hand. She glanced at it. Ever so faintly, she smiled. "I have your bag if you want to change."

"Yes, please."

He handed me the suitcase through the door.

"Here," she said.

"Thank you," I said.

She nodded and I closed the door. For a moment, I stood there. I could tell she hadn't moved away. Perhaps she was just eavesdropping on me to make sure I didn't set the place on fire or something, but I didn't think that was it. I think, like me, she was simply taken aback by the strange, brief intimacy we'd just shared, one woman helping another to get ready to be seen by people.

I took out a hunter green short-sleeved Kerrybrooke dress from my suitcase. It made me look like a housewife who was ready to entertain her husband's office buddies, and I figured the more feminine I looked the better off I'd be.

From the outer office, I heard the front door open and men's voices spoke low but intently to Lucy. Lucy's voice was little more than a whisper. It was a sure bet that they were talking about me, but everything sounded more urgent than it had before.

I finished dressing and stepped out into the office. Lucy and Eustace were standing by the front door. Two men I had never seen before stood there with them. Lucy held a piece of paper in her right hand.

They all stared at me.

"What is it?" I asked.

I didn't really need to ask though. I could see it on Lucy's face.

They'd found Amberly.

~ ~ ~

Despite the cutting winds blowing through the town square, it looked like the majority of the county had shown up. Men and women and boys and girls. Young and old. Families and clusters of rowdies. Some people looked well to do – some of the women looked as if they were on their way to church. Some looked poor and malnourished. They lined the street. They climbed up the frozen flagpole. They hung out windows and stood in the backs of trucks. They had all come to see me.

As Lucy and Eustace walked me out, no one spoke. No one threw a tomato or jeered or cursed. They all quieted down as if some authority figure had shushed them. They just watched me as Lucy marched me across the street. The only sound in the town square was the scrape of our shoes against the iced-over road and up the steps of the courthouse. The doors opened and more people stood inside, lining the hallways as we walked though, crowding the stairwell as we went up to the courtroom. In the courtroom, every seat was filled and people lined the walls shoulder-to-shoulder. Even the judge was already there, sitting at his bench, waiting for me to take the only empty chair.

Then Lucy turned me over to Bartholomew Oglesby.

~ ~ ~

It was a lynching.

Oh, I'd done everything they got me for. I'd fucked the preacher's wife, and then I'd run him over with a car and whacked him on the head with a chunk of wood, and I'd killed Amberly and buried her out in the desert. I'd lied and cheated and killed. I'd done it all.

But it was still a lynching.

They moved through it all so fast, I couldn't keep up. I didn't even try. I could only think about Amberly. They'd found her out there in New Mexico. They'd pulled her disintegrating body out from under the rocks and ants. My beautiful Amberly.

I really had killed her. She really was dead.

I let those men have their say. I let them make their speeches to each other about how terrible I'd been, about how I'd done such an awful thing. What did it matter what they said about me? I hated them for thinking that their opinion of me even mattered. What did it matter that I'd broken their laws? They didn't care that I had killed Amberly. Not really. Not as much as I did. No, they only cared that I'd killed Obadiah, that I'd humiliated and killed one of their own.

They asked me how I wanted to plead. The little defense attorney turned and looked at me. It was for me to answer. The stupid son of a bitch didn't even know how his client planned to plead. That's how seriously they all took my defense. They all just wanted to watch me squirm, to fight and beg for the freedom that none of them had any intention of granting me.

"Yeah," I told the court, "I did it."

You would have thought that I'd stripped down naked. People gasped, a gasp that started in the front of the room and swept to the back and down the hall and out into the square.

Josiah Pickett looked shocked, like he might need to hold on to something to keep himself balanced and upright. Oglesby just looked relieved.

"You're throwing yourself on the mercy of the court?" the judge asked.

I was mad. I was mad at all of them, even Lucy and Eustace. I was mad at the town, and the state – hell, I was mad at the whole Goddamn world.

I said, "I don't give a damn what you do."

The judge leaned forward in his chair, his face turning pink. "Well," he said, struggling for composure in front of the assembled audience. "I must say, in all my years on this bench I have rarely had to look upon such an obstinate face of moral degradation." He turned to Josiah Pickett. "Does the county have a sentence it would like to suggest?"

Josiah Pickett scrambled to catch the moment before it got away from him. He glanced at his notes, but they had not prepared him for this. He cast a quick look back at the room full of people waiting to hear him say something – especially at Lionel and Nathan on the front row. Then – and from where I was sitting I could watch it happen on his face – he had a thought. It was an obvious choice, really, the only way he could seize the attention of the people that was currently fixed on the judge and me. He said, "Given the unusually heinous nature of these crimes, your honor, given their root in the unholy sexual proclivities of the defendant, given the – the – the *attack* they represent on the God given roles of man and woman, and given that the state of New Mexico might want to challenge the jurisdictional sovereignty of the great state of Arkansas in this matter ... uh, it is with a sure heart and a steady sense of justice that the county strenuously recommends the sentence of death be imposed."

It was wordy, but it did the trick. It got the attention of everyone in the room. It got the attention of everyone outside. Before it was over, it would get the attention of the whole country.

~ ~ ~

The judge said he'd have to think about it for a while, so they hauled me back over to the jail. As Lucy and Eustace led me through the crowd, I didn't look down. I stared into as many of those faces as I could. Let them have their look. Young, old, ugly, mean, sad, sneering. I stared back at all of them. Some of them I'd seen before. Helen the waitress, the old man who ran the motor lodge. I couldn't really place most of them. Some women from the church, some regulars at Dub's, some people I'd seen around town. They'd all become indistinct now, hard to really see anymore.

But then we were almost to the jailhouse when I saw Claude. He stood by himself just beyond the edge of the crowd, just beyond the edge of the petty curiosity of the amassed townfolk. He stood there with his hands in his pockets. I wanted to wave at him, but I thought better of it. Might get him in trouble, and the fact of the matter was that he was the only one who'd been decent to me all along.

He watched them lead me into the jailhouse, and then as they shut the door I could see him turn and walk away. I like to think he went back to his theater and started a movie.

~ ~ ~

I lay in my cage and thought about nothing.

After a while, Lucy came to the door.

"Surprised?" I asked.

"You've surprised me every step of the way, Billie. I have to admit. I've been behind you the entire time."

"Think I should have fought?"

"I think you might have shown some repentance about murdering two human beings."

I flopped the crook of my arm over my eyes. "I don't have anything to repent to the men in that room for. What I did, I did to Obadiah and Amberly. It was between the three of us. I take responsibility for my part, but I wasn't alone in it. It took all three of us to make it what it was."

I moved my arm to see Lucy's face.

She stood with her arms crossed. She admitted, "I didn't think they'd ask for death. Even Leopold and Loeb didn't get death."

"Leopold and Loeb were in New York."

"I didn't know you planned to walk in there and tell them all to go to hell."

"Well?" I said.

"They're going to kill you, Billie."

"Think so?"

"Yes. Now I do."

I moved my arm back over my eyes. "Everyone you know is just a corpse waiting to happen, Lucy."

~ ~ ~

When it was time they took me back up to the courtroom. The crowds outside had begun to get restless, and people had moved around. The day was cold, and some stalwarts had started fires on the lawn rather than go home and miss the fun. I half expected them to spread out picnic blankets like I was the guest of honor at a church social. When I was led out, everyone stopped and gawked. This time, though, there was a sense of excitement. People smiled when they saw me, friends grabbed at the sleeves of friends so that no one would miss a chance to see me. It felt like a Goddamn movie premiere.

Upstairs in court, the judge got to make his speech. "I've been in my chambers seeking the counsel of God almighty," he began, and I pretty much lost interest in what he was saying after that. He would talk about himself, about how he had to weigh the public good and the laws of the land and all that, but I knew that the answer to the only question that I had would come at the end of this rhetorical masturbation. He finally brought it to a close a few minutes later, recapturing my attention when he said, "Therefore, I sentence you Miss William Dixon to death by electrocution."

And that was that. They pulled me out of there, threw me in the cage for a few days, and then hauled me up to the death house.

Chapter Twenty-Four

Dear William,
A few days ago we received a letter from a publishing company in New York City. A Mister W.F. Fawcett is interested in publishing your story in a book form. He says he has written to you about authoring your story or selling the rights to him, but you have rebuffed him on both counts. I know you know all the details of the proposed book deal.

Now he says that he will give us a portion of the proceeds if I can convince you to write the story.

I know what you must be thinking. 'Dear old mom comes out of the woodwork to try to make some money.' But, dear, I must tell you now that we have fallen on hard times. Burt's foot got run over a year ago by a gas truck, and he hasn't been able to walk right ever since. The money from this book deal would help us more than you could know.

Think of what it would mean to us. While I know I was not much of a mother to you, please also consider that your notorious reputation will be a blot on my name for the rest of my life. After the mistakes of my youth, I have tried to live my life as a good Christian woman, but now the papers speak of my firstborn daughter in the same breath as Ruth Snyder and Belle Gunness and Bonnie Parker –

They say worse, that you lured that preacher's wife into types of immorality that I cannot bring myself to even write about.

This is a stain on me, on my children, your brother Earle, and your sisters Katherine and Pearl.

So please consider signing the contract which Mister Fawcett has proposed. If you have admitted to your crimes as the papers say you have, if you have been so defiant as to spit and curse in the courtroom as they say you have, then you might just as well write this book. If your family must pay for your notoriety, then we might just as well profit by it as well.

Forgive me if any of this sounds cold, but I think if you consider things from my position you will see that you owe me some recompense for the dishonor you have brought to me.

Cordially,
Your Mother

Chapter
Twenty-Five

Dear Mother,
Go to hell.
Your Daughter,
Billie

Chapter Twenty-Six

Today's the day.

The warden sent a preacher in to talk to me this morning. He was a jug-eared old man with liver spots the size of polka dots. Clutching a Bible with both hands, he told me, "Despite everything you've done, the Lord still loves you. The blood of Christ covers all sins, even yours. You can still be saved, Miss Dixon. Jesus has not turned away from you, and he will not give up on you. But at the moment of death – at that very moment – it *will* be too late."

"I appreciate you coming to see me," I said. "But I don't think so."

"You must understand," he pleaded, "that although you are going to die in just a few hours, your soul is going to live forever. Where do you want to spend eternity? Down in a hell that will be far worse than any pain you feel in that awful chair? Or up in the heavenly realms, with the Lord of all creation?"

"You really think there are invisible worlds out there?"

"This book here says that there are."

"I know it does."

"Miss Dixon ... if thinking you're smarter than God led you to this room, then what good has your obstinacy done you? Shouldn't you grab holt of God's hand before he draws it back forever?"

I leaned forward. "Sir, if I could believe for one second that there was really a God in heaven, then I would kiss his ass all day long to get me out of this fix

I'm in. But I can't believe it. Not even for one second."

That preacher meant well, I think. He's just an old ignoramus who's made a living out of selling redemption to a bunch of dupes. Maybe the only way he could pull that off was to convince himself that it was all true. But I know better. I've always known better. You make your choices and those choices have consequences. That's all there is to know. The rest of it – religion and redemption and all that – it's all just moonshine.

The preacher left shaking his head.

After that, the warden and a couple of jailers came in with the matrons on loan from the women's prison to ask me if I had any requests – did I want to eat one last meal that wasn't pig slop? Did I want to fire off a last will and testament?

I didn't care about any of that. I don't have anything to leave anyone.

~ ~ ~

I forget how long I've been on death row. A few months at least, but it's hard to keep up with it when every day is the same and you never see the sun. It doesn't really matter how long it's been. It's been long enough that everyone has had their say. The newspapers have published their editorials, the politicians have made their speeches. Some folks wanted me dragged out to a tree and strung up the minute the judge handed down his verdict. Others think it's pure evil to electrocute a woman, no matter what she's done. There was a group from some university in New York that wanted to come down and make a big show of rallying around me, but I told them to go to hell. I didn't want to spend my remaining days crying for the newspapers.

I have gotten some pretty good mail in here, though. A lot of it has been misspelled invective and creative name-calling. My favorite was "The Whore of Sodom." I asked one of the matrons if she'd see to it that "Billie Dixon, Whore of Sodom" was put on my tombstone. She got a kick out of that. She even called in a couple of the other matrons so I could say it again.

I got some fan mail, too. One guy wrote to tell me that he'd never met a preacher he didn't want to kill. And I got two love letters, neither of which had return addresses, both from women. They were both a couple of screwballs, but one of the letters was pretty steamy. She said she kept a newspaper clipping with my picture next to her bed and used it to help her pleasure herself. The other letter was more romantic. She said she understood why I had killed Amberly, said it was the most beautiful thing she'd ever heard of, said it made her cry every time she thought about it. I wanted to write her back and tell her that I hadn't killed Amberly on purpose, but it wouldn't have done any good, even if I'd had a return address. No one believes I killed Amberly on accident. Sometimes I'm not even sure.

The cell here is a windowless cinder block that somehow stays damp all the time. I've had a cough off and on the whole time I've been here. The food is scraped together from whatever the hogs won't eat. Arkansas is a hell of place to die.

I don't know what time it is now. They'll be coming for me soon.

~ ~ ~

Late this afternoon, a matron came in to tell me that I had a visitor. I knew who it was without asking. There's only one person it could have been.

I felt bad for the way I look. I'm thin and pale, and my gray prison dress was probably fashioned from old coal sacks. But I did want to see her.

The jailers took me outside. The yard is just a patch of grass in the middle of a dirt lot, but at least it's outside. Over the side of the high wall, I could see the crown of a tree starting to bud. Today was warm, but the sun was going down and a chill was starting to settle. I stood there and felt the last rays of daylight on my face.

A moment later the door opened, and she stepped through.

"How have you been?" I asked.

Lucy looked good. She wore a black dress with black heels and carried a small white purse with a crescent cane handle. To my surprise, she was also wearing lipstick and some make-up. She looked damn good. A little sad maybe, but damn good.

She said, "I've been fine. But you, how are you?"

I shrugged. "It's ... terrible. I don't know what to say beyond that. They want it to be awful, I guess, and they've succeeded. This is an awful place."

She nodded.

"Have you ever been here?" I asked.

"No. First time."

"Well, thank you for coming to see me."

She nodded. "I felt I should."

"How's Eustace?"

"He's fine. We're being replaced, did you hear?"

"No," I said. "What happened?"

"The Picketts. Lionel made it known that he was going to challenge Eustace in the upcoming election, so I went to see him. I told him that if he'd stop running us down around town, we'd quietly retire. I saw no reason to subject Eustace to public humiliation."

"I'm sorry," I said. "I feel like that's my fault."

"No, your case was just an excuse. As soon as Lionel came home from the war, our days in office were numbered. We only got the job because the last sheriff died and no one wanted to take over. I was the secretary and Eustace was the guard at the jail. The boys who would have naturally filled the position had gone off to fight the war, so the town entrusted it to us until they got back. All things considered, I think I did a good job. If I was a man, I'd get to keep it. I'm not."

I nodded and watched the sky. The amber sun would be sinking for another hour or so before the horizon swallowed it up, but I knew I wouldn't be outside to see it. I watched the sun disappear over the prison wall, and that was it. That's as close as I'll get to a final sunset.

"Doesn't it make you angry?" I asked.

"What?"

"That you don't get to keep the job?"

"I can lose the job and be angry, or I can lose the job and not care. It's easier to live with it if I choose not to care."

She looked at me, her eyes still as guarded as they had ever been. She was so different from Amberly. Everything about Amberly had invited me in. Lucy wasn't cold, but everything about her kept me at a distance.

"Do you think we could have been friends?" I asked her.

She blinked at that, genuinely surprised by the question, and parted her lips as she struggled for an answer. "I don't know, Billie."

"I don't mean now, after all that's happened. I understand how you must see me now. What I mean is, is there a version of this world where we could have been friends?"

Lucy took a deep breath and said, "The world is what it is, Billie. I've spent my whole life trying not to imagine something better. Dreaming only hurts."

"Not for me. Not here. Not today. A couple of dreams are all I have left. So dream a little, just for me."

She gave me a smile like a small gift. Then, quietly, she said, "You and I in a different world? Who's to say what could have happened."

I smiled.

She lowered her eyes.

I asked, "Have you ever been married?"

Still looking at the ground, she said, "No."

"Do you think you'll ever be married?"

"No."

The door opened. "Ladies," a guard called out. "You need to wrap it up." Then he leaned against the doorway, smoking a cigarette and glancing absently at the sky.

She looked at me.

Quietly, I said, "I know this can't mean much, coming from someone like me in a place like this. But I wish we could have been friends. I wish I'd met you before I met... I just wish I'd seen you more clearly." The guard in the doorway coughed up something solid and spit it in the dirt. I shook my head. "I wish we could have been friends. I wanted you to know that."

Lucy lowered her head and put her hand to her mouth. When she raised her head, she said, "Thank you for telling me that, Billie."

"You're welcome."

She nodded. "I should go."

The guard threw his cigarette on the ground. Lucy smiled at me and nodded. Like the sun disappearing over the prison wall, this is all I would get.

"Thank you for coming to see me," I said.

"Of course," she said.

They led us back inside. The matron took me by the arm. A guard opened a door for Lucy. Beyond it was the long hallway that led to the front of the prison.

"Thank you again for coming to see me, Miss Harington," I said.

Lucy stopped at the door. "Claude's open for business regularly now," she said. "I'm going to help him run the Eureka. I thought you'd like to know." Then she turned and walked down the hall.

~ ~ ~

And that was that. Since Lucy left, I've been sitting here with nothing but the echo of my thoughts bouncing around my head.

It's just me.

I wonder if that old preacher I talked to this morning was right about there being a life after this one. I doubt it. All I am is the brain thinking these thoughts. Once it's fried and in the ground –

The sound of keys clang down the hall.

Hinges scream as a gate opens.

Footsteps are coming my way.

The cell door opens and they all crowd in. The warden and the guards stand against the wall as the matrons pull me to my feet and shackle my hands. No preacher. I guess they figure I've had my chance.

They lead me out. A short hallway, some wooden stairs. The groan of wood as we go down to the basement.

A little room. They sit me in a metal chair next to a wooden table. A couple of matrons come in with a bowl of water and some scissors. They cut my hair with the scissors. I watch clumps of it plop down in my lap and slide off to the floor.

Another matron shaves my head with a straight-razor. Cold water runs down my spine. She nicks my scalp and blood drops in my eye.

The women leave and the men pick me up and

take me down the hall.

The room is smaller than my bedroom in LA. The chair is against the wall. It's a rickety looking thing. They push me down on it. This is the room I'm going to die in, surrounded by these men.

They strap down my hands and feet. I shut my eyes. I don't want to see what's happening. I don't want to cry. Not for these sons of bitches.

The warden reads some legal bullshit. I hum loudly and shut him out. They must think I'm crazy.

The warden asks me something. I keep humming, drown him out, but he steps toward me and shouts, "Do you have any last words?"

I keep my eyes shut. I hum. I don't want to say my last words to these men. I said my last words to Lucy.

The warden steps away and says something to the man with the switch and as he's about to burn my brain out of my skull I picture Lucy Harington's face one last time and I think *That is one hell of a lady.*

Thank you for reading.
Please review this book. Reviews help others find New Pulp Press and inspire us to keep providing these marvelous tales.

If you would like to be put on our email list to receive updates on new releases, contests, and promotions, please go to NewPulpPress.com and sign up.

About the Author

Jake Hinkson is the author of several books, including the novels *Hell On Church Street*, *The Posthumous Man*, and *The Big Ugly*, the short story collection *The Deepening Shade*, and the essay collection *The Blind Alley: Exploring Film Noir's Forgotten Corners*. His work has been translated into French by èditions Gallmeister. Born in Arkansas and raised in the Ozarks, he currently lives in Chicago.

www.newpulppress.com/